THIS CHRISTMAS

J.R. Hart

A NineStar Press Publication

Published by NineStar Press
P.O. Box 91792,
Albuquerque, New Mexico, 87199 USA.
www.ninestarpress.com

This Christmas

Printed in the USA
First Edition
December, 2019

Print ISBN: 978-1-951057-93-0

Also available in eBook, ISBN: 978-1-951057-95-4

Warning: This book contains sexually explicit content, which may only be suitable for mature readers, mentions of depression, alcohol, and homophobia.

Alex Ross can't catch a break when it comes to Christmastime. With a long history of bad holiday experiences—like getting rejected under the mistletoe or playing referee to his mother's divorce—he's just trying to survive it.

New in town and a stranger to everyone, he plans on ignoring the holiday altogether. That would be easier if his ridiculously cheerful new neighbor would cool it on the Christmas hype. Nicholas is annoying and loud. Worst of all, he's also impossibly attractive and nice to everyone. It's getting harder for Alex to deny his interest, especially when Nicholas leaves Christmas cookies at his door and wages a snowball fight against him on the coldest day of the year.

Can Alex open up to him and get into the holiday spirit before he endures another ruined Christmas?

Alex Ross can't catch a break when it comes to Christmastime. With a long history of bad holiday experiences—like getting rejected under the mistletoe or playing referee to his mother's divorce—he's just trying to survive it.

New in town and a stranger to everyone, he plans on ignoring the holiday altogether. That would be easier if his ridiculously cheerful new neighbor would cool it on the Christmas hype. Nicholas is annoying and loud. Worst of all, he's also impossibly attractive and nice to everyone. It's getting harder for Alex to deny his interest, especially when Nicholas leaves Christmas cookies at his door and wages a snowball fight against him on the coldest day of the year.

Can Alex open up to him and get into the holiday spirit before he endures another ruined Christmas?

Chapter One

Christmas Spirit

Peppermint. Everywhere Alex looked, on every shelf, peppermint surrounded him. Before Thanksgiving had ended, someone sneezed red-and-white stripes throughout the grocery store. Most of the year, Alex was indifferent to peppermint. He didn't have a personal grudge against the flavor, not really. At Christmas, however, indifference became loathing.

What was the point of basing an entire season around one specific flavor profile? He didn't get the excitement of mint, the mad rush to stock up as if the ingredient were scarce. Calculating an extra ten minutes into his routine to account for peppermint mochas being all the rage and the long lines accompanying the seasonal drink? Not particularly enjoyable. Personally, Alex preferred peppermint in the summertime, stirred into a glass of lemonade. In the current season, chamomile tea was a far better option, particularly in Omaha, which may as well have been a frozen wasteland. As he loaded the chamomile variety into his cart, he looked at the peppermint tea beside the others on the shelf again. *How many people buy that thinking this is the only time it's available?* It wasn't a limited holiday tea. *Do people really not know this?* Peppermint tea was right there, on the shelf, year-round. But somehow, no one touched the tea in the summertime.

Alex found it a little scary how some crafty marketing on the part of a few national giants—a few food brands—could push peppermint to the forefront of everyone's minds, convincing them the one flavor was a requirement for a good Christmas. Marketing alone could make one flavor of tea, available year-round, fly off the shelves during the right time of year. "Madness."

While he could deal with the fascination—darn near obsession—with peppermint products surrounding him in the aisles, he couldn't stand the chaos and overcrowding Christmas caused. He hadn't realized he'd been standing in front of the tea for as long as he had until a woman bumped him out of the way—no "excuse me" or anything—to reach the tea. He watched her snatch up several boxes of the very same peppermint green tea he'd rolled his eyes over. He wanted to be home badly, instead of at the store.

"You know they sell that stuff all year?" Alex asked. *Stupid question.*

She replied with a glare, then added two more boxes to her cart before wheeling away.

"Okay, then."

Comfort food. Alex stalked away in search of comfort food. Not comfort food in the way most people would define it, but rather the food he personally found most comforting. Starting with the obvious item—the largest jar of peanut butter the store had to offer. He wondered how offended the cashier would be if he grabbed a pack of plastic spoons and tore into the jar now. He needed comfort. Moving to a new city, right before the holidays? Yeah. He needed peanut butter. Bread wasn't important.

His preference was to eat the substance straight out of the jar, where the creamy—never crunchy—mass could squish in and fill the emotional void left behind from the tension of shopping at Christmastime, the internal stress from packed aisles crowding in on him, overwhelming him. He scuffled his feet along the floor, head low, set on trying to avoid eye contact with any other shoppers.

Alex wasn't in the mood to conjure the polite, Christmassy grin he was forced to give the other shoppers. The store piped in annoyingly saccharine, cheerful Christmas tunes, and the music was starting to give him a headache. *I hate Christmas.* He hadn't always, but right now, he couldn't bring himself to like the holiday. He attempted to elbow his way around a cookie display with shoppers crowded around. When he couldn't manage to get through the crowd, he maneuvered between, reaching an arm in under someone's elbow and above another shopper's wrist. He grabbed two boxes, tossing them unceremoniously into his cart.

Too late to put the cookies back, he noticed the words "candy cane," printed on the label. With the crowd, there was no way he could reach in and put the packages back. What about the season necessitated peppermint added to the cream-filled center of a sandwich cookie? He didn't understand the need there. "What's wrong with plain Oreos?" No one heard his question. Which was fine—he hadn't wanted an answer. He should have ordered his groceries online, he realized in hindsight. But, he was here now. Leaving the store empty-handed didn't make sense.

Saccharine tunes came through the speakers, crooning classics surrounding shoppers in the store. "On the eleventh day of Christmas, my true love gave to me..." From the next aisle, he could hear a voice singing along.

The stranger didn't bother to hum or sing along quietly as most other shoppers did. Instead, he made his presence known. "Eleven pipers piping." His voice was booming and excited. "Ten lords a-leaping!" Whoever he was, he was getting into the music, holiday cheer annoying Alex from an aisle over. As Alex grabbed a box of cereal off the shelf, he caught a glimpse of a garish Christmas sweater, a peek of beard, and lips moving along to the song. *Of course.* He was desperate to get out of the store. The sooner he finished shopping, the sooner he could leave the festive hellhole and take a nap. His mind flitted to the booze aisle. Alex considered alcohol to be a decent enough solution for getting through the holiday season. Unfamiliar with the store's layout, he wanted to find where he needed to go so scanned above him for a sign. He didn't see it. Instead, he turned and saw a lone box of peppermint bark on an endcap. He debated grabbing some.

If the candy was any good, it might make up for the peppermint overload the season itself had. Besides, it was the last box. The fear of missing out overwhelmed him. Peppermint wasn't *all* bad, even at Christmas. He reached his hand out to grasp the box as a large hand wrapped around the other side.

"Oh. Oh gosh." A man, the one who had been singing, judging by his festive, candy-cane-striped sweater matching the one Alex had seen through the aisle divider, looked at him. "You can have it," he said, but he didn't let go of the box. He was offering with the hope Alex would decline and let him have the box. Alex could barely stifle a groan as he looked up at him. The guy looked a little too into Christmas in the sweater, and his obnoxious attire was a lot to take in.

Alex wasn't short. He rarely had to look up at anyone. But this festive giant towered over him, so he let go. "I don't even like peppermint bark," Alex said. "Take it." The last thing he wanted was to get on this guy's Grinchy side over a box of candy he didn't actually want.

"What?" The man in front of him stared, aghast, mouth open, jaw dropped in an exaggerated way Alex had only ever seen in movies, as if Alex had somehow personally attacked him with the statement. "You're not a fan? It's a holiday staple, man!"

Alex resisted any and all temptation to tell him, "I'm not your man." He hated when people said things like that, so overly friendly, as if they knew each other, but he bit his tongue. Instead, he tried to hide his basket behind him, remembering it was full of peppermint cookies, not that he'd wanted them either. He worried the man had caught an eyeful, but then again, did he really care? He wasn't on trial here! Apparently, what *was* on trial was whether or not he liked peppermint bark. Christmas and everything related to the holiday was on his last nerve; that was certain.

"No," Alex said. "I am not a fan of peppermint bark. All it is is mint and chocolate. Go get a box of chocolate mints in the candy aisle—exact same thing, but the stuff sits there year-round, and nobody's trying to convince you you'll have the worst Christmas ever if you don't have it."

"Uh…" The man cocked his head to one side.

Alex considered he might have come off a little too strong, and for a moment, he was embarrassed by his mini-tirade about how awful the holidays were. He didn't back down though. In fact, he realized he'd made a good point. Like he'd told the guy, he could go to the candy aisle if he needed chocolate and mint so badly. "It's true," Alex said. Frustrated with himself for getting sucked into the marketing, he was thankful some crazy person in a sweater had come along to snap him out of buying the peppermint bark—or worse, into the peppermint delusion—when he didn't want it.

"It's not the same!" The man protested. "This has a pepperminty crunch! It's magical! I can't imagine not loving peppermint bark!" Alex quirked an eyebrow and backed away slowly. "Or Christmas! Or candy canes! Of course, I bet that's because my mom set me up with the whole naming me after Saint..." Alex shook his head, muttering "Merry Christmas," and went down an aisle before the man could finish explaining how his mother's love for Christmas somehow translated into a desperate need for peppermint. He didn't have the energy for any of this. Instead, he stalked away, grabbing a bag of chocolate-dipped pretzels—sans any sign of peppermint— before checking out.

Nicholas finished his sentence under his breath, mumbling, "Saint Nicholas...you know, the Jolly ol' Santa Claus." One person wasn't about to ruin his holiday spirit, even if the cute redhead did cut him off and walk away.

He felt both victorious and a little guilty in the moment, having taken the last box from the man. For a second, he considered chasing after him and giving him the box, already regretting his choice to take them. "Merry Christmas," he said, watching the guy stalk away, ripping a bag of pretzels from a shelf in a huff as he made a beeline for the checkout. *He's cheery,* Nicholas thought, but he pushed the sarcasm from his mind. "Oh. Well." He considered the man didn't deserve them, but reigned himself in from his judgment of the guy. He wasn't going to let this grumpy stranger get him down. Not during his favorite season.

His cart was overflowing—fresh fruit for pies, shortening and flour for the pie crusts and his famous Christmas cookies, some nuts, boxes and boxes of butter, and more sugar than appeared sensible—all for his Christmas treats. Everything in his cart was for making others happy, ingredients he would use to bake gifts for his friends and neighbors, all things he would use to make their holidays brighter. But the peppermint bark? That particular treat was entirely his to enjoy, the one thing he took delight in having without feeling the need to make the sweet from scratch. Peppermint bark was the one item he had no intention of sharing with anyone. He put the box into his cart, then looked at the list in his hand. Though he'd crossed everything off, he found himself double-checking regardless. Better to discover he missed something while he was at the store than to get home and realize there was a key ingredient he'd have to scramble back for midrecipe. The phrase "checking it twice" popped into his head, and Nicholas found himself humming about Santa Claus coming to town, all the way to the checkout.

Alex hadn't finished his mental list, hadn't bought half the staples he decided he needed to stock his new apartment, but he was over shopping and the forced cheer. Loading the items in the trunk of his car, he bristled against the cold. Even the interior of the car was cold. The heat on full blast wasn't enough for him, coming out icy at first. He sat there shivering, waiting for warmth. He wondered if his heat worked properly. In LA, he'd only had to use the setting once. The rest of the time, the dial was either set to air conditioning or off completely. He held his hands up by the vents—he wasn't used to this Midwest chill—and rubbed them together for any bit of warmth he could get. "Getting gloves would help, Alex," he said, snarking to himself in his otherwise empty car. "And now you probably look absolutely ridiculous talking to yourself in a very clearly empty car. Way to go." He turned to the backseat, which had tinted windows. "At least now if someone saw how crazy you look, they can assume you're talking to someone in back, right?" Alex sighed and shook his head. *Yeah. You look ridiculous.*

As the air inside the car warmed, he stopped rubbing his hands together, settled into the seat, and turned the radio dial. He tried to get any station not playing Christmas music. His car was old, and he didn't have the luxury of an aux cord or a CD to keep him company. Not finding what he wanted, he gave up completely. "Great. Frickin' great." Right when he didn't think he could get more miserable. He didn't know any of the stations in Omaha yet. Regardless, programming stations in a frigid parking lot was a waste of time. He grumbled to himself and shifted into reverse.

The knock on the window jarred him out of his thoughts. He yanked the gearshift back into park, then lowered his window an inch. The glass was frosted over and fogged up from his breath. He wasn't sure what to expect. The Jolly Giant from inside the store was high on the list of things he'd never thought to consider, and Alex blinked at him, not entirely sure what to say.

That didn't stop the guy. He leaned down, peering through the small slot Alex had given him to speak through. "Hey! Looks like we parked next to each other, stranger."

This man was cheerful to the point of sending every *stranger-danger* signal in Alex's body flaring. No one should ever be so chipper, he thought. Alex found himself wondering how much sugar—or liquid Christmas cheer—the man had already had that day. Alex wanted to close his window and block out the flurries starting to drift into his car. He desperately hoped to cut the conversation short. "Yeah. It, uh. It's quite a coincidence, I guess. Have a good day." Alex's finger smoothed across the window button and he started to close it. *Who knocks on a stranger's window to comment on where they parked?* For a moment, Alex wondered if he'd dinged the guy's car with his door, and this was a friendly way of calling him out.

"Wait!"

Alex released the button, lowering the window again the tiniest bit and peering skeptically through the crack.

"I've got something for you. I felt bad about taking the last box. Seems like you could use a pick-me-up." Nicholas held the peppermint bark up, rocking the box gently back and forth in his hands.

This guy clearly doesn't let things go, Alex sighed and lowered the window the rest of the way. Was this some kind of trick? "Thanks, but I don't have any cash on me."

"No! I didn't mean for you to buy it. I meant as a gift. Consider this an early Christmas present." He kept grinning, and for a moment, Alex wondered if he was on one of those weird hidden camera shows.

"Seriously, you don't have to. I mean it when I say I'm not fond of peppermint bark, and I get the feeling you'd enjoy the stuff a lot more than I would. I was, uh... I was buying it for a friend. I'll find them a different gift." Alex was an awful liar, and he imagined the man could tell by how much he overexplained the situation instead of saying "no thanks." He kicked himself for the dishonesty. Every lie was written on his face, and this guy was just being nice. Still, Alex was only a little ashamed. *He should feel weird, not me.* After all, Alex was simply trying to get home, and this guy was practically forcing peppermint bark on him.

"Please take it. I hope your friend enjoys it!" He had a brilliant smile and a complete lack of concern or confusion, as if he was willing to accept Alex's lie for whatever reason. He passed the box through the open window.

Alex didn't have a choice but to accept the gift and place the box on the passenger seat. If he didn't, the whole situation would be weirder than this already was. The man had already chased him down in the parking lot—or maybe not chased, if they were truly parked beside each other—and offered him candy until he'd lied trying to refuse the gift. They'd passed awkward. Refusing again would have made Alex look downright *strange.* "Thanks, uh..." Alex trailed off. He didn't know this guy, didn't know his name or anything about him. He was quite literally taking candy from a stranger. Doing so was a slap in the face of anything his mother had ever taught him; that was for sure.

"Nicholas. I'm Nicholas," he said. His cheeks were rosy, kissed by the cold air and turning them a soft pink like his nose. They peeked up over his beard, nice and round. He looked cold, in spite of the fingerless gloves and the scarf he had on, both bright red with white stripes. Or white with red stripes. Alex couldn't be certain.

"Oh. Right. Like Saint Nick. I should've guessed," Alex said, shaking his head. "Thank you, Nicholas. Seriously." He actually meant it.

"No problem. Have a Merry Christmas!" Nicholas said.

"Thanks. You too." Alex gave a small wave and rolled his window up. After he pulled away, he realized he'd never offered his own name. "Stupid Christmas spirit," Alex muttered, but he couldn't help smiling at the box on his seat. If nothing else, he could take the kindness as a sign Omaha wasn't a bad choice after all. At least the people were nice, if not completely weird. At this point, he would have taken any good thing as an indication he'd made the right choice to move, even if the situation was half-baked.

For a moment, he wondered if he were hallucinating. A jolly man who was so into Christmas, generously gifting sweets to a complete stranger in a grocery store parking lot? Nicholas? *Really?*

Chapter Two

Too Much Holiday Cheer

Had anyone been in the kitchen with him, Nicholas might be embarrassed by how loud he was singing, but his Christmas pop playlist was too perfect for him to resist. He couldn't help but sing along with the music. Not enjoying the music to the fullest was downright wrong during the holidays. By *enjoying*, he meant singing at the top of his lungs.

Not that he was ashamed. Whoever might have been spending the holidays with him might have been equally enthralled with the music and would have been happy to sing along too. He wouldn't know. He was alone in his empty apartment, as usual around this time of year. Christmas pop was a far cry from the kind of thing he would have listened to with his mother or grandmother. They would have wanted traditional Christmas songs. With both of them gone, the thought of listening to the music they would have chosen was too painful. At least if one of the songs they would have adored came on, the pop twist would make him far less prone to crying. Now, he only wished there was someone in the kitchen to take his mind off his loneliness.

There wasn't, and Nicholas pushed the thought out of his mind. The last thing he wanted to think about was being alone at Christmas. *Way to be completely pitiful.* He shifted his focus back on the caramel mixture bubbling on his stovetop as his hips swiveled and swayed in time with the music. He scraped down the sides of his pan with a green spatula.

Pies lined the countertops, ready for gifting. Jade and Brandon would each get a pie for sure. They were his best friends, their lives so interwoven he couldn't imagine this stage of his life without them. He'd have to figure out what to do with the other four he made. He hadn't originally intended to make so many pies. He'd planned on a few, but he couldn't decide which flavors to make, so he baked them all. Now, as he looked at the row of desserts on his counters, he second-guessed his choice. In hindsight, narrowing the number of pies down to match the number of close friends he actually had might have been a smarter plan. *Oh well, I can always eat one or two of them myself.*

He'd filled most of the open surfaces in his apartment with other baked goods. There were more than enough to take some to every person in the hall he lived on, and he hadn't made the fudge or caramels yet. *Too late now.* He'd already bought the ingredients, so there was no stopping, even if he knew he'd made more than was necessary for his plans. He snapped his attention back to the caramels, focusing on them so they wouldn't scorch.

Making Christmas treats kept him busy when everyone else he knew had holiday plans. Jade had Veronica to watch Christmas movies, to listen to music, or to go Christmas shopping with. He was happy for them most of the time. Brandon had his girlfriend of the moment, too, but Nicholas couldn't recall her name. If she stuck around past the holidays, he'd ask Jade again.

Nicholas eyed his thermometer, double-checking the temperature of the caramels and stirring them again. With his knee, he managed to work open a drawer nearby and grabbed a small spoon to taste test. There was no real need to. He'd been following the recipe to a *t*, and he'd made these every winter since he was a teen. Every year, they turned out exactly like they should. That didn't mean he couldn't have a taste, and Lord knew he wanted one.

"Nicholas, you get that spoon out of your mouth this second!"

"Yes, Ma." He rolled his eyes, but he couldn't suppress his smile. "Sorry."

"If you stick that back into the pot, knowing full well I'm taking those to the Hendersons, I will smack you upside the head with my wooden spoon." She wouldn't. The threat was empty and they both knew it. This was part of the tradition. They baked. Nicholas taste tested. His mother told him to stop picking at the sweets. And then they laughed and sang and continued baking. She didn't need to worry. He knew better than to cross-contaminate her sweets or use a tasting spoon for mixing, but that was part of their banter.

"Hey, Ma, what if we chopped cranberries into this?"

"Into caramels?" She raised an eyebrow skeptically.

"Can it hurt?"

"Heck, go for it. In our batch." She smiled at him. This was part of baking together, bouncing ideas and seeing what worked. They tried a little bit of everything. He found out the hard way cranberry

caramels were abysmal. Peanut butter ones, on the other hand...

The one thing in the world conveying Christmas magic to him—more than the music or the snow or anything else—was a kitchen full of baked goods. His fondest memories were of time spent there with his mother, how she'd tell him, "Mind the thickness," as he rolled out gingerbread to hand cut the dough for houses, rubber bands wrapped around the sides of the rolling pin to be sure he didn't get the dough too thin, and then mixing icing together to pipe on.

They'd spent most of his childhood using trial and error, as they baked their way through generations of family pie crust recipes, on a mission to determine the flakiest one. Ultimately, a truly flaky crust required a splash of vodka. Vodka, it turned out, incorporated into the dough like a liquid but burned off to leave little pockets where the moisture had been, pockets of air that flaked when he cut into the crust with a fork.

His grandmother had been the same way, a natural baker. Together, they had made traditional desserts from around the world using recipes they found in old church cookbooks or gathered from close friends and family. She'd never have admitted the truth to anyone but Nicholas, but a few favorites were from cookbooks she'd found at garage sales, instead of ones passed down through their family. He remembered most of the desserts they'd made over the years, everything from the cheeky Better than Sex dessert to a strange strawberry "salad." Nicholas had the cookbooks on his overstuffed bookshelf. Almond horns from an old German recipe, little powdered sugar cookies from Mexico... They weren't in his regular rotation of Christmas desserts, but one day he might have the guts to incorporate them, to take a whack at them on his own.

"Nicholas, dear, rummage through the box over there, could you? I see some spiral-bound ones. They look promising." Even in the morning, the day was a scorcher, so hot steam came up off the asphalt street, strange low-lying mirages promising relief. Beads of sweat dripped down his back. Didn't matter. Gran had told him to, and he did exactly as she said.

"Looks like we've got the, uh, Strawberry Hill Methodist Church Cookbook and a book on bread making from Betty Crocker."

"Get that Methodist Church one. I think Margaret went there before she passed, rest her soul, and if it has her pineapple salad recipe, we're going to the store before we go home."

Nicholas could see it now. Any of the old church cookbooks were her favorite, but he wondered if this was going to turn into a journey on par with the Great Milnot Search from years ago when they'd found a cookbook from the 1960s calling for an ingredient called Milnot. And then no store in the area carried filled evaporated milk, only plain evaporated milk, resulting in a four-hour drive south to Kansas so they could grab a few cases at the closest store they found. "Sure thing, Gran." He grabbed the cookbook and checked out, treating her to a glass of lemonade from the child-led stand in front of the sale.

As soon as she was in the car, she was flipping through and dog-earring pages. "That ruthless witch! There's no pineapple salad in here." She shook her head and kept flipping as he drove her to the next sale. "Well, at least this raisin pie recipe looks worthwhile. Make a note, dear. We'll have raisin pie for Christmas this year." Never mind that Christmas was six months away, and never mind that he had no way to make a note while driving. Sure as anything, they'd have the raisin pie.

The memories hit him hardest, the thoughts of the time he spent sharing treats with the people he loved most. His family would bake until there was no room left to put the final product anywhere, exactly like he had done alone this year. Then, they packaged the desserts up and delivered them to family and friends during the holidays. The childhood tradition led him here, to start his own baking traditions, if only to honor their memories. Now he baked treats for his apartment hall. He'd done so since he'd moved in two years before, when he'd entered the grad program. He was determined to see the holiday baking through for as long as he lived here. He hoped his passion would strike the same chord with someone else who lived nearby, someone with equally strong memories from their upbringing, and they'd decide to carry on the torch. Regardless, he was sure he'd do what his family had done and deliver treats to the entire neighborhood someday.

Nicholas poured the caramel mixture—still molten and bubbling—into a lined baking dish with great care, doing his best to avoid any burns. Anything he couldn't scrape from the sides of the pan, he'd enjoy later. He was certain he'd pick off every last bit for himself before washing the dishes in the morning. Dusting sea salt on top of the caramels, he watched it settle nice and coarse, glimmering crystals sitting on top of each piece, accented by the twinkle lights stretched across his ceiling. He wasn't sure if his mother was right or not about salt enhancing the sweetness, but who was he to question her? He followed her instructions unwaveringly.

Despite how he'd exercised great care pouring the molten caramels into the pan, he let himself get careless with the bits stuck to the side of the pot, burning his fingers. He was too impatient to let the unset caramel cool. Nicholas licked at the spatula carefully, trying hard not to burn his tongue as well. The flavor was lovely, the right balance of sweetness to the charming hints of salt.

The fact that he hadn't spurred some sort of sugar shock by tasting every treat he made had to be some kind of Christmas miracle. Most of the year, he was very healthy, eating a balanced diet and watching his portion sizes, hitting the gym a few times a week, the whole nine yards. In December, all bets were off. His body was left to adjust to the mountain of sweets he piled on during the month, left to deal with the soreness he'd face in January after his sole workout for the month was stirring and decorating. *Maybe this year I should at least attempt the gym too. Can't hurt.*

A quick glance at the clock reminded him it was nearly midnight, but he wasn't anywhere close to being ready to stop for the night. He was too full of cheer. Or sugar. He was also too unwilling to head to his empty bed in his dark apartment. Besides, he'd had a few too many cups of peppermint tea early in the evening. He found himself poring over recipes and debating if he should start with the fudge next or the cookies.

The fudge was quick and easy, a simple recipe his aunt had given him before she passed away. The cookies, however, took more effort. He opted for the crisp, buttery cookies. They were brilliant when they turned out right, getting rave reviews every time. Making them alone was less exciting, but he'd deal with it. Unless...

Nicholas dusted his hands off on his apron and pulled out his phone. First, he texted Brandon. They'd known each other since fall, when Brandon had moved into his building, and they'd grown close, mostly because they'd debate various topics. Brandon loved to argue, and Nicholas was happy to oblige, taking the opposite stance of whatever perspective Brandon held, if only for the sake of discussion.

Half the time, they were important topics—recent Supreme Court battles, news stories, politics—and whether or not their true opinions were from the same side of the aisle wasn't relevant. The debates were simply that: debates. They'd set aside personal feelings and argue against their true beliefs from time to time, if only to get the other riled up. Tonight, if Brandon came by, they'd go for a lighthearted topic. Pies versus cakes, maybe, or salted versus unsalted butter.

However, Brandon didn't respond to his invitation to come bake, so Nicholas was back where he'd started.

Even late at night, he didn't have to worry about time with Jade. He hit send anyway. From anyone else, "Hey, you up?" may have sounded like a booty text, one to make Jade's girlfriend worry. Coming from him? Not a chance in hell anyone would think that.

Instead, Jade texted back in the snarky way she always did: "I am now." Nicholas rolled his eyes, but then he smiled. The *now* implied he'd woken her, but the speed at which she'd responded meant that wasn't anywhere close to true. Jade was the heaviest sleeper he knew. Her response meant he'd interrupted a horror movie marathon. Halloween might have been long over, but Jade never slept on a good scary flick. Regardless, she was busy.

He texted back, skipping the invitation to bake, and instead asking: "Want to help me deliver these treats tomorrow?"

"Depends. Are there any for me?" As if she didn't know the answer!

He laughed, tapping a message in response: "Duh. Friend tax, right?" This was the first time she'd help him deliver the treats, since she'd moved in at the beginning of summer. Her girlfriend was in the same program Nicholas was. While he liked Veronica well enough, inviting both her and Jade for dinner regularly, his real connection was with Jade, specifically. She was like a sister to him. The bond had fallen into place mere days after they met.

"How can anyone be so cheery this late at night?" Her response was quick.

"I don't know. Don't question it. Don't question my love for you, J! Don't!" His texts were getting increasingly giddy, and she sent back emojis with hearts and crying laughing faces.

"I'll never question you." Her text was sweet, but her next left him dejected. "See you tomorrow, lover boy." So much for baking help.

It didn't matter. He shifted his focus to the peppermint and the cold chill in the air outside and the pop songs playing through his apartment. It didn't matter if he was alone for the evening; he had plenty of reasons to be happy. He was determined to make the most of his night and smile through the intrusive thoughts about loneliness trickling in. He tried his hardest to keep himself as cheerful as Jade assumed he was. With the taste of one last cup of peppermint tea on his tongue, he aimed to adjust his mindset, trying for happier thoughts.

How could anyone be less than hopeful in December? He reminded himself that this was a time of magic and miracles. All he needed to do was believe in Christmas spirit, and he'd be fine. Maybe doing so was childish, but to Nicholas, focusing on positive daydreams and memories were the fastest way out of his solitary thoughts.

One final text to Jade confirmed the time they'd meet up the next day, and then he switched his focus back to his playlist, turning the music up. "These cookies won't bake themselves," he said. No one was listening. He could talk to himself or sing as he worked and no one would hear.

He pulled a mini candy cane from the pocket in the front of his apron, tucked it into his mouth, holding the candy between his lips, and flicked his tongue over it. His pocket was nearly empty, and he grabbed the box from the cabinet, tipping more candy canes in until he'd filled it. During the holidays, candy canes were the primary staple of his diet. He set his focus on the next recipe, gathering the ingredients he needed: flour, sugar, butter, maple syrup...

He had a few versions of the cookie he would make each year. Most of them contained cute, sugary Christmas tree sprinkles. Some had crushed candy canes. But his favorite had a secret ingredient, one few people expected, one he kept stashed in the fridge every year, hidden in the back and wrapped in a grocery sack as if someone might bust into his apartment and go searching for the secret ingredient before he was ready to reveal it. He knew everyone on his hall, aside from a couple of newcomers. Getting to know everyone, being friendly with them all, made deciding who was open to the surprise he was offering much easier. He went through his mental list and opened the package, laying the bacon strip by strip into the pan.

An essential ingredient, bacon made the cookies taste better than sprinkles or peppermint, one secret and unique to his cookies alone. Bacon tilted the balance of the rest of his mostly sweet array of treats into the savory category, if only for a moment. Plus, bacon made for a nice surprise. Good Christmas gifts should hold an element of surprise. This was it, the special secret ingredient intended for his neighbors to start their holiday season off on the right foot.

Nicholas began singing louder now, lost in Britney Spears's rendition of a Christmas hit as he let the bacon sizzle. He'd deal with the errant splatters of grease in the morning. For now, he used the handle of his spatula as a microphone, bopping around the kitchen between rolling out cookie dough and flipping bacon so it wouldn't burn.

Alex poured himself a glass of whiskey and sank into his recliner. The Christmas music bubbling out into the hallway from his neighbors' apartment was overwhelming. "Must be a real party animal," he sighed. Of course, he hadn't been invited. He'd only been in the apartment for a few days, so he wasn't slighted. He hadn't expected to do anything this year, didn't figure he'd end up getting any invitations anywhere. His lack of expectation didn't make sitting alone sting any less. He reminded himself as he took the first few sips: anything beat being in LA.

"Get out!" Alex's mother was screaming, and for a second, he wasn't sure if she was yelling at him or at his stepfather. It would make sense if she were yelling at him. He'd kissed his best friend. His best guy friend. Was it really a stretch to think she'd found out somehow and decided now was the time to kick him out? No. Not in the slightest.

The words didn't make the target of her anger clear enough, but the ring hurled halfway across the room at his stepfather's head said plenty. The way she turned to Alex and sobbed into his neck said more. He knew he should feel a little guilty for not being honest with her, and for his sense of relief over the end of her marriage, especially if the situation distracted her from what he'd done, but he didn't. Not really. Call it self-preservation. He rubbed her back and glared at his stepfather. Or, soon-to-be ex-stepfather. Why wouldn't he? Letting the distraction hide his mistakes was the right thing to do in the situation. As soon as she pulled away to yell some more, he pulled out his phone and texted his stepsister. "They're splitting up. Again." He followed up with a second text. "Pretty sure they're done for good this time."

Who screwed up so badly in December, of all times? Alex hadn't been in the room to hear the words that ended their marriage, walking in with gifts two seconds after the damage was already done, but knowing those two, the whole situation started from a petty statement that got out of hand. Pettiness was par for the course with his mother and his stepfather. A small comment like "That's not my favorite dress, but it looks all right," or "Can you please get your feet off my coffee table?" could escalate into an all-out war.

For Alex, whatever sparked the fire was irrelevant. What mattered was that he was standing in the middle of his mother's living room a couple of weeks before Christmas, looking back and forth between them, and wondering if he still had the receipt for the flask he'd bought for his stepfather, Marty, or not, and wondering if he could return an engraved flask in the first place.

Christmas alone was supposed to be better than how he'd spent the holiday the year before. Being alone wasn't what he'd hoped for, but anything had to be better than that Christmas from hell. He had sworn to make things better for himself, determined to change the trajectory of his life, but apparently he hadn't worked hard enough at it.

Being in Omaha was a good start. Being here alone, however, wasn't good or free in the way he'd anticipated. He picked at the leather of his recliner, one of the few pieces of furniture in his bare apartment. His application for the grad program had been accepted in the middle of the year. He'd never expected the sudden acceptance letter, figuring he'd be waitlisted until fall. When he saw Christmas start to go downhill fast back home, worse than the year before, he took the leap of faith and accepted right away, moving in the first day the apartment was available. His studies wouldn't start for a few weeks, and they offered to hold the apartment, pending a deposit, but he couldn't wait. He'd been so fed up with things in California that he hadn't bothered delaying his move. His acceptance letter was the catalyst for everything in his life right now: for the cross-country drive, for the few nights he'd spent in his car, for the week he'd lived in an extended-stay hotel waiting for the apartment. Anything to dodge the chaos back home, to keep himself from having to be there.

"Are you sure you have to go now?"

"The program is in high demand, Mom. If I don't accept and get my butt out there, they'll give my spot to someone else." Liar.

"But before Christmas? They can't let you come in January?"

"Mom, if I had a choice, I'd wait. It's...with class starting in January, they need to know now."

"So tell them now, and then go out after Christmas," she said. The lie was logical enough. Mostly because he could do exactly that. He could stay in town, leave right after the holiday, drive to Omaha, and get there in time for his start date of January 14th.

"I'm sorry, Mom. The apartment is available tomorrow. I'm already making them hold the place as it is." Everything out of his mouth lately was a lie. Every single thing from *"Yeah, Mom, she's very pretty"* to *"The apartment won't wait for me."* He couldn't help lying. She'd never accept the truth. As they headed into the holidays, the thought of her wailing in her bedroom on Christmas morning

became less and less appealing. The countdown to Christmas was already sending her into enough of a tizzy. The more time they spent together, the worse she seemed to get.

He couldn't handle the stress.

So, he lied. "I'm going to go pack, okay? Maybe by next year, I'll be able to come back for a visit at Christmas, and we can do something fun."

Making a habit of lying wasn't the best idea—not like the school lie was the only one he'd told his mother lately—but he didn't have a choice. Keeping secrets from her seemed safer than telling the truth. His landlord had told him there was no rush. He had time. But the idea of spending Christmas at home with his mother in emotional anguish and going to the same Christmas parties *he* would be at? He felt a little sick at the thought.

All the anguish of past Christmases, the pain from years before, and his mad rush to get to Omaha had left his new apartment devoid of any Christmas spirit at all. Why get a tree or hang lights or put up tinsel? No one was there to enjoy the decorations, and even if they were, he didn't care. "I don't like Christmas," he muttered. What was the point? Christmas was 80% marketing, 15% family time, and 5% outdoing everyone around. It wasn't about actually enjoying the holiday. The only Christmas-like thing surrounding him was the music piping in from under the door, sounds from someone else's party. That, and the peppermint bark from the stranger, Nicholas, which he'd come home and immediately stuffed into a cabinet.

He held his whiskey in one hand, wondering why he'd bothered with the glass and hadn't gone straight for the bottle, and his phone in the other, scrolling for a Christmas playlist and picking the first one he could find, some randomly generated mix of cheerful songs. If he couldn't join his neighbors, he could at least drown them out with loud music of his own.

Shuffle had other things in mind. Being less than kind to him, the first notes of Elvis's "Blue Christmas" sputtered from the weak phone speaker. "Figures," Alex muttered, closing the app and returning to the near silence of his apartment.

He waited for more than an hour, having another glass of whiskey and silently begging the music to fade, begging for the raucous singing and noise to stop for the night. As each minute ticked by, the music sounded louder. Was it really? Or was the volume change all in his head? Maybe the alcohol or the isolation of being alone in a dark apartment was making him imagine things. The music sounded so loud, though, and he considered his neighbor really was turning up the volume. "Ugh."

He finished his glass of whiskey and sulked to his room, pressing his pillow to his ears. The muffle of fabric wasn't anywhere near close to enough to drown out the noise, and the stuffing would never be enough to quiet his mind, swirling with exhaustion, frustration, and fear. He might have considered attempting to smother himself with the pillow if he wasn't so certain the grad program could be a positive change for him, if only he could get through the stupid holiday. Besides, smothering himself would be ineffective. He wondered how his idea would even work. If anything, his brain would sense the tangles of suffocation creep in and he'd let go out of instinct. He was stuck on the most pathetic train of thought.

Alex tossed and turned, giving up on sleep and walking back into the kitchen in a huff, pulling the box of peppermint sandwich cookies, which he'd accidentally bought, from the cabinet. "Why'd they have to screw with a perfectly good cookie?" he muttered. Vanilla ones would have been fine. Then, he poured himself another drink. Clearly, his neighbors had no plan to end their festivities anytime soon.

Had his cybersecurity degree granted him the ability to hack into his neighbor's streaming service and shut down the whole thing, the night might have been redeemable. Not that hacking was his skillset. Until now, hacking wasn't even an interest. In the meantime, the music droned on. Unless the noise stopped, he wasn't going to be able to stop the cycle of intrusive thoughts and seasonal loathing either.

The minutes ticked by slowly as he poured himself one more drink, then one more after. At one in the morning, the noise was too much to bear, the sounds coming from under his door slipping into his ears and embedding into his brain. "Shut up," he said aloud to his apartment. His brain was now in a tipsy fog. "Shut up, or I'm going to shut you up myself." The idea wasn't half bad.

He stood up, bathrobe loosely belted as he stalked into the hall, letting his door slam behind him as he stomped across the carpeted floor in his bare feet. He still had his drink in his hand. In the hall, he listened to the music, clearly coming from one door in particular, the apartment next door to the one across the hall from his own.

Lifting his hand, he gave a sharp knock. He'd been overhearing their party for hours now. No one came to the door, but the off-key singing continued from the other side. He didn't recognize the song or the artist, but it didn't matter. Who could tell the difference between artists singing some vaguely annoying sugary pop song far worse than whatever the original they butchered might have been? His neighbor had the worst taste in music on the planet, Alex decided. By comparison, "Blue Christmas" wouldn't have been a bad choice after all.

"I don't get how you can stand her voice," Sean said.

"It's catchy!" Nicholas insisted to his boyfriend, but he conceded, turning the volume down a little, singing quieter before stopping altogether, focusing on the road and trying not to sing along, trying to stifle his excitement.

"You know what's catchy? Something else." Without asking, Sean unplugged the aux from Nicholas's phone and plugged in his own, starting up the first slow notes of a song with a far different tone. Catchy? Not exactly. The harshly screamed lyrics over melodic violins was certainly a unique contrast, but Nicholas definitely didn't enjoy his music, by any means. They had different tastes, and he accepted that. He'd try harder to find a compromise next time. For now, he settled in and listened to Sean's favorites.

Nicholas was in too deep on the Christmas pop playlist. He couldn't resist singing along now that the playlist had cycled back to current hits, finally unashamed and unwilling to hide his passion for pop. He'd hidden his taste in music for too long, tried to shake it from his system, but now he was free to listen to whatever he wanted. No one was there to stop him. He attempted

Ariana's signature high notes as he piped icing onto the cookies, stacking hollowed-out ones onto flat ones to make a secret chamber for the fillings. He wasn't sure if he was successful in hitting the notes, but who cared? The freedom to sing obnoxiously without judgment was the sole perk of baking by himself.

The loud pounding on the door immediately after, though, embarrassed him. He tried to stifle the blush on his face before opening the door. Obviously, someone *had* heard his failed attempts, which he assumed sounded more like a deranged goat than anything. He paused the music, stopping midverse, and wiped his hands on his apron, trying to calm himself down. It occurred to him he was being unruly—he hadn't noticed until that moment how loud he'd been.

If they were upset about his noise level, he hoped turning the music down would stop the knocking. Mostly, he didn't want to face them, completely embarrassed by the situation. They didn't seem like they were going to stop knocking, so he didn't have a choice. "Coming!" he hollered toward the door before yanking it open and almost laughing. The man from the store, the grumpy one whose name he hadn't caught, stood there. "I am *so* sorry. Was I being too loud?"

"Were you—" Alex scoffed. "Do you have any freaking clue what time it is?" he slurred. "People are...people are trying to slee— Wait a second. You're the uh... You're the... the guy with the um...uh...the..." He stood at Nicholas's door, his own turn to blush with embarrassment now. He stumbled on his words, clearly caught off guard by seeing Nicholas on the other side as he stood in the hallway, intoxicated, wearing nothing but a bathrobe and boxers, which Nicholas noticed as the man used one arm to hold his robe closed a little bit tighter.

Nicholas could smell the whiskey on his breath as he leaned against the doorframe to steady himself. "The peppermint bark," Nicholas reminded him. He was attempting to save him from a few more seconds of awkward verbal stumbling. "I'm Nicholas." He said his own name in hopes the man would introduce himself this time. Instead, nothing. A blank stare, head tilted to one side. "Listen, I'm sorry. I got carried away with the music and didn't realize how loud I was being."

"Okay."

"I wasn't trying to disturb you," Nicholas said.

"Okay," he repeated, standing there staring at him.

"Can I make it up to you somehow? Would you like to come in? I have pie." Nicholas tilted his head toward the inside of his apartment. He was trying to sound sincere, mostly because he was. He meant his apology.

"No," Alex's face twisted in confusion. "Who the heck invites a stranger inside in the—" Alex swayed, caught himself on the doorframe, then blushed. "—middle of the night for pie? Are you even okay? Like, that's not normal." Nicholas wondered if Alex would remember this conversation in the morning. He had trouble not smirking. "I want to go to bed. I don't want pie."

It was Nicholas's turn to say, "Okay." He wasn't stopping Alex from returning home and going to bed.

"Is there any kind of, y'know, timeline on your guests leaving, so you can turn the music down, or..." Alex peeked around Nicholas. He must have realized the apartment was empty and stopped in his tracks. The music was already off. His tirade was rendered completely and utterly pointless before Nicholas had ever opened the door.

"What guests?" Nicholas smirked. "It's just me. Me and my pies. And cookies. And candies."

Alex furrowed his brow again. "But the music... I thought you were having...uh...a party, and...and...I'm sure this is the right apartment," he said, muttering the words to himself. Nicholas could hear as well as Alex could. There was no other music, no other apartment to visit to ask for quiet.

"I promise. I'm here alone. And like I said, I'm very sorry. And I do want to make it up to you. Do you want to at least take a pie with you?" Nicholas was darn near pleading at this point. He convinced himself his plea came from his own guilt about being inconsiderate, but if he stripped that away, the honest truth was he was sad over how he'd spent the whole evening on his own. Company, including drunk, agitated company, was better than no company at all.

"What?"

"I asked if you wanted to take a pie with you. I've got...uh...peach, caramel apple...ooh...and pecan! You don't have a nut allergy, do you?" Nicholas asked.

"I'll pass. I don't eat pie with strangers at two in the morning," Alex said. He started to turn away, but then he whipped back around. "Are you always like this?"

"Like what?"

"So festive. And so insistent on people eating. First, you give me peppermint bark, now you're offering me pie."

"No," Nicholas said, but then he corrected himself. "Not always. I uh... I didn't know we were neighbors. Also, I didn't realize how loud I was being. I'm hoping you'll forgive me."

Alex, he realized, was barely listening. Instead, he looked Nicholas up and down, apparently losing his train of thought in an alcohol-induced haze. Nicholas paused his apology, letting Alex take in the full outfit. He didn't limit his festive apparel to the top half of his body. He was decked out all the way, down to the candy cane socks. Quite literally, he was wrapped head-to-toe in seasonal apparel. "I get really excited about Christmas," Nicholas explained. He pulled a mini candy cane from his apron, unwrapping it.

Alex watched him, quirking an eyebrow. "I didn't realize Christmas was a personality trait," he mocked.

"Oh! Gosh, sorry," Nicholas said. "I'm being rude again." Or maybe he wasn't the one being rude, he considered. He couldn't argue with Alex there. He was probably overdoing it, at least to a stranger's perspective. He reached into his apron pocket, pulling out another mini candy cane. "Want one?"

Alex shook his head. "No. I'm going to bed. If you could keep the noise down, I'd appreciate it."

"Sure thing," Nicholas said, but Alex was already turning on his heel and walking away, back to his apartment, robe flapping around him. He struggled with the knob, cursing under his breath as he turned it one way and then the other. "You locked out?"

Alex didn't answer, continuing to turn the handle before it finally opened. "No. I'm not." He stalked in and slammed the door. For a moment, Nicholas stared at the closed door between them, then he shut his own door and leaned against it. Looking down at his apron and socks and then across the room at the baked goods littering his apartment, he was almost ashamed of the overindulgent way he'd been acting. Just as quickly, he pushed the thought from his mind. He'd turn the music down, but he wasn't about to let a grumpy, tipsy Grinch stop him from spreading holiday cheer.

Nicholas sat down at his kitchen table, crumbling bacon into the center holes in his cookie, topping them with another cookie to hide the bacon inside. These were his all-time favorite Christmas cookies. If the mysterious peppermint-bark stranger—who still hadn't mentioned his name—had stuck around to try one, maybe he wouldn't be quite as grumpy. His cookies weren't peppermint. As long as the guy wasn't vegan or something, Nicholas couldn't imagine he'd find a way to dislike them. Nicholas was counting on the idea he'd like them, when he delivered some to him the following day, the same way he'd deliver them to everyone else who lived on his hall. There was a small chance the treats would go in the trash, but Nicholas wanted to try. Even without knowing him, Nicholas could tell he needed some kind of pick-me-up. Everyone deserved a good Christmas, especially if they didn't realize it themselves.

"You have to...no, look! You need more frosting." Mike's hands overlapped his, and Alex tried not to blush. He shouldn't be having such an intense reaction to his best friend, but he couldn't help how he felt. The proximity was killing him.

"More? I've used half a tube!"

"Dude, it's going to keep falling apart. I'm telling you. You gotta use more, or it'll keep falling down."

Alex sighed and laughed, shaking his head. He reached for the tube with one hand, letting Mike support the graham crackers that were supposed to be a gingerbread house. Slowly, carefully, he piped frosting between the cracks. He glanced up. "You think I used enough?"

"Yeah. That's definitely enough," Mike said. He let go, and Alex's house fell in on itself in a heap.

"Or...maybe not?" Alex cocked his head to one side, laughing. "So much for trusting you on that being enough."

"Aw come on, it's not...okay, yeah, it's that bad. If the theme were ancient ruins, you'd be killing it." That was one thing about Mike. He was forever confident, or at least he came off like he was, and Alex couldn't resist him.

As Alex lay in bed, he couldn't pinpoint the song he was humming, the one caught in his head. Until he got to the chorus, he couldn't pinpoint why the tune was so familiar. Then he realized. The song was the same poppy hit he'd been obsessed with the Christmas before, and the one Nicholas had been singing. Back before he'd gotten so deep in his head, back when he still thought Christmas meant possibilities and maybe a shot at love. Back when he actually wanted to make an attempt at a good, very Merry Christmas.

Chapter Three

Ding Dong Ditch

"My God, Nicholas." Jade turned back and forth, eyeing the sweets. Nicholas knew the tone well, her shock and concern pretty evident. "I don't think I've seen this many baked goods outside of a bakery before. I swear, if you weren't dead set on becoming an engineer... How late were you baking last night, anyway?"

"I lost track a little after one," Nicholas said. He rolled his eyes back, trying to remember the last time he looked at the clock. Recalling his neighbor stopping by and pounding on his door, he knew he'd turned off the music sometime around then. From there, things blurred together. "I'm not sure. Probably three or four? I finished these last night"—he gestured to most of the kitchen, then turned toward the fudge—"and finished these this morning."

"Exactly how many armies do you plan on feeding with this? We going to throw in a couple navies as well?" She snorted and shook her head, pulling on the food-safe gloves Nicholas insisted upon.

"Only this floor," he said. "Maybe the one above us if we have leftovers. Put six caramels and four pieces of fudge on each of those plates." He nodded at the plates stacked near her, festive plates his recipients could reuse, he hoped. He'd bought them on clearance the year before.

"And have what, four thousand of them left over?"

"It won't stretch as far as you think," he said, looking up from what he was doing—placing a dozen cookies on a plate—to bark instructions, then tone himself down a little. She was helping. Even if she *was* being hypercritical of his overindulgence. He covered his plate carefully with cling wrap.

"You know you have fourteen caramels there," she said, cocking her head to one side. "And you said four cookies, not twelve."

"I know. The ones you're working on need less. Four cookies, six caramels," he replied flatly. Jade was always transparent, and now was no exception. He knew she was digging, asking questions to find out why this particular tray was getting more. Not wanting to get into his reasoning, he focused on numbers. There was no need to tell her why he was piling this tray so full. Besides, he felt absolutely ridiculous. He wasn't sure why the tray being perfect mattered to him in the slightest. The food would inevitably end up in the trash. The man was a little—no, a lot—rude to him. But it *did* matter. He picked up a pie from the countertop and put it in the middle of the tray, arranging plates of treats around that center focus.

"You didn't mention adding a pie to these." Jade was no longer assembling treats. Instead, she leaned against the counter, drumming her fingers against her cheek, fishing for the details she wanted.

"You're not supposed to add pie!" Nicholas yelped, worried she was catching onto his overloading a little too easily. He'd hoped she wasn't paying attention. "Stop worrying about my tray! Focus on the plates." He took a deep breath, then said, "Sorry. I...I didn't mean it like that. I...I owe someone an apology. This one gets a few extra things; that's all." He waved a hand dismissively and prayed his explanation was enough to satisfy her curiosity. Of course, knowing Jade, his dismissal would only open the door to new questions.

"Pfft, okay, if you can call an absolutely packed tray of sweets a *few* extra, sure. What'd you do? Run over his dog? Burn his house down? Kick his mom?"

"No."

"Break his nose? Steal his parking spot and then back into his Lexus? Love him and leave him?" She smirked. "Come on, you know I can do this all day. Tell me already."

"No, I...um. I got carried away with the music last night, and a neighbor stopped by right in the middle of 'Snow in California' to ask me to turn the song down. I'm trying to make things up to him," he sighed.

"I'm assuming you turned it down, right? And knowing you, you apologized about twelve times and—wait, it's Christmas, so you must have also offered him a mini candy cane once or twice during your conversation." She narrowed her eyes. "You *already* apologized. Don't you think this is a bit much for an apology?" Raising an eyebrow, she stepped closer and inspected the tray, lifting up the edge of the pie plate and setting it back down, then letting out a soft hum. "Unless he's really, really cute and totally your type." Jade's coy grin said plenty.

"I don't know what you're talking about," he said.

"Don't you? Tell me, was he tall?"

"Nobody's tall compared to me."

"You know what I mean. Red hair? Blond? Reddish-blond? Don't act like you don't have a type, Nick."

He ignored her, pulling out two candy canes from his apron pocket. "Want one?" he held the candy out to her as he attempted to unwrap his own one-handed.

"Oh, no. No, no, no. You're not getting out of telling me so easily," she insisted. "Was. He. Cute?" She caught his eye and stared him down, ready to force an answer from him if he wouldn't offer one up willingly. "Do not make me hurt you." Her threat was empty, and they both knew it.

He looked down at his feet and took a long, slow inhale and drawn-out exhale, as if by making breathing take long enough, she might forget she'd asked him a question in the first place.

"Yeah. I mean, he's a little cute. I guess. I don't know." Nicholas knew his ears were turning red talking about the guy, so he squirmed away to focus on the treats instead. He took a card from the drawer by the refrigerator and scrawled a handwritten note quickly. No matter how hard Jade tried to sneak a peek, Nicholas shielded his card, so she couldn't make out a single word. He caught her glancing toward the typed label he'd created for the other plates, a generic message saying the sweets were from a Secret Santa.

As much as he loved Jade, he wasn't about to give her the full story. Not until he talked himself out of whatever this crush might be. To his relief, she stopped prying and finished the plates she was working on, without bringing up the mystery recipient again, until they were nearly done filling them.

"Are you going to at least tell me about him?"

"What's there to tell?" Nicholas asked, pulling at the collar of his shirt. "You've *heard* my Ariana. It isn't quiet. He was grumpy and a little tipsy. I don't know anything else!" He bit his lip and crossed his arms. "He's new here. I think."

"Ooh, new and mysterious. And cute, right? I haven't seen you like this in...well, a while. Anyway, I like him already," she said. "What else?"

"I don't know anything else!" he insisted. He realized suddenly that he really wished he did.

Alex stayed in a deep sleep, an alcohol-and-fatigue-induced slumber, until his doorbell buzzed and jarred him from his dreams. He woke up not knowing where he was at first, too new to his apartment to fully get his bearings. As he looked around the room and pulled himself together, he remembered. A glance at the clock beside him told him it was midafternoon. "Jesus," he muttered. The fact that he'd slept half the day away hit him hard. "How much did I drink?" Alex wiped away the haze clouding his eyes and the drool on his cheek, while walking to the door in boxer briefs and trying to wrap his robe around himself as he did.

He hadn't started classes yet, and he didn't have a job, so he didn't have the slightest idea who might be at his door. He hadn't met anyone, hadn't made any new friends at all. "Probably the wrong apartment." Then he considered his landlord could be checking in. Alex peered through the peephole. No one was there.

He considered going back to bed until he could wake himself up more, but instead, he cautiously opened the door, glancing from side to side to see if anyone was walking away. He'd taken too long to get there. Anyone who might have actually been there to see him must have given up. There was no one in the hall, just chatter down past the corner, but then a door across from him swung open, and a few others opened too. The woman in the doorway across from him—he hadn't met her yet—

glanced down and picked up the plate in front of her door. Giving him a small wave, she smiled and retreated back inside.

Alex glanced at his own feet. At almost every door around his, there was a plate with ample treats for the holiday season. At his own, there was a tray. Nicholas's empty doorway confirmed what Alex was already certain of: the cheerful man, who lived nearby and had insisted on giving him food at every turn, had succeeded and was the culprit of this random treat appearance. As he closed the door behind him, he muttered, "What is his weird obsession with feeding people?" He shook his head and put the tray on his table to inspect the offerings.

He'd only gotten a quick glance at the plates left at his neighbors' doors, but the pie was the most obvious difference. Clearly, he'd gotten more food in general: tall cookies stacked up with a wreath design on top, a plate of caramels and one of fudge, handfuls of mini candy canes. The whole setup was a little overwhelming. Nicholas had clearly invested some serious time preparing the sweets. Balanced on the far corner of the tray was a box of the same peppermint tea Alex had mocked at the store, a note taped to the top.

> *I know you said you didn't care much for peppermint bark, but maybe you like peppermint in other forms? This was the only tea I had. I hope you like it, anyway—it's my favorite! Sorry for keeping you awake with all the noise. I have a little trouble resisting a good Christmas song. Hopefully, you were able to get some sleep, but I'll keep the music in check from now on. Maybe these will help you forgive me? Happy holidays!*
>
> *—Your Neighbor in 14B (Nicholas)*

Nicholas had drawn a small sketch of a Christmas tree beside his name on the handwritten card. Alex stared at the tray, wondering how many people Nicholas assumed he lived with. There were enough sweets to feed a large family, but certainly too much for Alex himself. There was no way in heck he'd be able to eat an entire pie and all of the cookies and candies Nicholas had given him. Not without gaining a significant amount of holiday weight. For a moment, he thought about throwing the entire thing into the trash to resist the temptation to eat everything himself, shoving down his loneliness and fear about being in a new place. Eating his feelings was the worst possible plan, and he hoped to limit that.

For now, he really wanted a cookie. He lifted the edge of the cling wrap to get one, and as he lifted one, two others came with it. He shook them to try to dislodge them before he realized they were stuck together on purpose. Nicholas, for whatever reason, had cemented them together with frosting in a small stack. He smelled them, getting hints of maple syrup and the overpowering powdered sugar scent of the frosting. "At least it's not peppermint," he said, chuckling to himself, biting the edge of the cookie and tasting the hints of maple his nose had picked up on. The frosting added more sweetness beyond the taste of syrup. As he took another bite, he pulled back. Something savory fell from the cookie. It didn't taste bad, but he spit the filling out at first, if only because of the surprise. "Bacon?" He sniffed at the cookie, then broke it apart. A small opening in the center was stuffed to the gills with tiny pieces of it. Without the element of surprise, the salty-smoky flavor was magical, a break from the sugar overload that lined the tray. After one more bite, he decided he liked the flavor, enough to make him grab two more cookies. "Screw it. I'll go to the gym later." The on-site workout room was an added perk of the building he lived in.

"Pretty sure we got everyone," Jade said, leaning against the wall of the stairway corridor. She was panting, and Nicholas struggled to catch his breath too. "If you had warned me deliveries would be so exhausting, I'd have said no." She laughed, and he shot her a look, smiling right after.

"Come on, it's not that bad." It *was* that bad. The mad dash down the hallways was more tiring than he anticipated. Even with her summer 5K participation, they were both out of shape for the season, and the hallways of their apartment building weren't conducive to a sprint. They'd carefully placed each plate, one in front of each door, then they'd worked their way backwards, ringing doorbells and running down the hall as quickly as they could, hiding in a small corridor before anyone could find them.

They'd waited, catching their breath and trying to recover from the rush of the whole activity. Nicholas hoped everyone would get the plates without them being seen at all. If they returned to his apartment now, he feared they'd be caught in the act. It didn't matter. He was the only one without a tray in front of his door. Either way, he was sure almost everyone knew he was the mastermind behind the gifts by now.

He thought about the typed labels, the way they were so vague, reading, "From your Secret Santa." Or, all but one, which had the handwritten note revealing who he was. If Jade was right—and Nicholas didn't want to entertain the idea she was—he only let Alex know who he was because he was attracted to him, grumpy as he may be. No, it wasn't that complicated. The extra sweets were merely an attempt at an apology.

"So nobody knows you're leaving the food?" Jade asked.

"Nobody knows," he said. "Wait, I lied. I think a few people do. I'm pretty sure most people who were here last year have some idea or another." He sighed and leaned against the wall. "I haven't exactly come out and said, 'Hey, I'm the Crazy Christmas Guy!'"

"Yeah, I'm sure your door isn't a dead giveaway, Nick." She was the only person allowed to call him Nick, the only one he didn't cringe at when they said it. Sisters, even chosen ones, had special privileges.

She was right too. His door had to be a dead giveaway. Wrapped like a gift, his apartment door was covered in tinsel and glittery ribbon that shed sparkles onto the hallway carpets. By contrast, the grouch across from him had nothing. Not a wreath or a string of battery-powered Christmas lights like some of the other doorways on their hall. No Menorah, like his next-door neighbor, who had one embroidered on a banner and hung on the door. There wasn't a shred of tinsel or a fleck of acknowledgment a holiday was approaching. *He just moved in,* he reminded himself. *Maybe he's not always grumpy.*

Judging by the door, Nicholas wondered if the man didn't celebrate at all. He hoped he hadn't offended him. *Too late now.*

"Does he know?"

"No," Nicholas lied. His note had been very incriminating, but Jade would only keep picking if she knew.

She nodded. "You should try telling him. Maybe he'll want to chat up the hottie who baked for him."

"Shut up," he groaned, but he couldn't suppress a smile. *Maybe, but I doubt it.*

"I think anyone who was home got theirs already," Jade said, peeking out the corridor and taking note that most of the people who lived within view of their hiding spot had collected theirs. Only a few plates sat untouched.

"Yeah, it's probably safe," he agreed, peeking over her head. His new neighbor's door was around the corner. Nicholas couldn't see his apartment from where he stood, so there was no way to know if he'd gotten his gift yet or not. It didn't matter, he convinced himself. He ducked out of the corridor on a mission to return to his apartment, Jade in tow, for hot chocolate.

"Hey, Mom? You want to make slice-n-bakes?" Alex nudged open the door to her bedroom. Her lights were off, the room dark, curtains drawn. She didn't move. "Mom?"

"No," she finally said. "Go ahead."

"Not without you, Mom. I won't ruin our tradition," he said quietly. "How about I get some light in here and see how you're feeling?" He opened the curtains, studying her as she pulled the blanket up over her head. He couldn't remember the last day she showered.

"I'm tired, sweetheart. You go ahead and make them, and I'll eat some when they're done."

It wasn't like he didn't know how. They were slice-n-bakes! Sure, he'd burned those a few times, but that wasn't the point. These were the easy ones, the pre-sliced ones that went straight from the package to the baking sheet. Mumbling, he baked them, getting half the pan a little too dark.

"Hey, Mom. Brought you some cookies."

She didn't move. "Thanks." An hour later, she still hadn't touched them.

Maybe there was something inherently awful about leaving in the midst of someone's depression. The deep sense of guilt about lying to his mother nearly every day cut through him. His guilt was stronger on the days where he sent a text to check in instead of calling. But could he blame himself? She'd gotten better—therapy had helped—but burdening her with his own issues, particularly a sexuality crisis she'd never approve of, was too much. He'd comforted her through the end of her marriage as much as he could, while struggling with the loss of his friendship, his crush, and his self-esteem. The stress from various problems became too much to juggle, too high a burden on one man's shoulders. Especially, he knew, because he only enabled her. The only way they could both heal was for him to leave.

So he left.

Mostly, spending another Christmas pretending didn't seem fair to him, his mother...anyone. He couldn't pretend to be normal. She couldn't pretend to be happy. If he was gone, neither of them had to pretend at all. He might have stayed, if every conversation with his extended family didn't crush his spirit a little more. All of the stress led to him applying for the program in the first place.

Getting as far away as possible seemed like the only fair solution. The second he'd been accepted, jumping on the offer made sense.

Alex tried to shake all of the worry and second-guessing from his head. He wasn't getting anywhere by thinking about how he might have made the wrong decision. No. That didn't help. Instead, he stood in the stream of hot shower water falling on him, trying to wipe the dream from his head, the memory of his mother in bed, unwilling to get up for the smallest of traditions the year before. The hot water was a stark contrast to the winter wind howling on the other side of his apartment windows.

He was still trying to wake up, to warm up, to do anything the water might help him with. Winter was never quite so cold in Los Angeles. The cold whip of wind and the flurries falling gave him a clear enough idea of the frigid temperature without him ever having to set foot out there. He wondered how he'd survive the cold chill of winter. Did he feel this way because of the gray, overcast skies? Or his dreams and guilt? Despite the sense of newness on the horizon, he was down and depressed. Blaming the weather was easier than admitting the truth.

The weather wasn't the only culprit, and he knew it, but no one else had to. Being alone had to be better than trying to fake a smile for his mother. Being alone had to be better than the arguments with his extended family, the pressure they put on him to fit inside a certain mold, the many questions he faced at Christmas dinner, and every holiday between then and now about when he'd find a girlfriend and settle down. *Surprise, everyone! Won't happen. Not like I've ever told you why, or made excuses about how busy school is and how I haven't found the right person.*

Instead of embracing the idea that things could only go up from rock bottom, more than ever, Alex was stuck. He was letting himself spiral. The transition to Omaha from Los Angeles wasn't nearly as easy as he imagined. Being away from the pressure was a positive, but the lack of any support system altogether? The whole thing was harder than he'd anticipated. Without friends, without any real connections, the holiday rapidly approached. No icy chill outside could compare. The sense of being alone, of total isolation, closed in on him in his apartment. The chill of his loneliness had nothing to do with the wind.

Alex leaned his head back against the shower wall and let his thoughts wander. They flitted back home, to whether or not he'd made the right choice.

"Al, you done with this?" His grandfather called him Al more often than not. Of course, he did. Anything to convince himself Alex was more like him.

"Hmm?" Alex looked up from his bed to see the old Sears catalog in the back of his drawer. "Oh. Uh. No. I can throw it out." Alex was trying to play it cool, reaching for the glossy catalog.

"No need. I've got it."

Alex watched his grandfather leave, with the catalog he'd so carefully hidden behind his dresser tucked under his arm. Please don't open it. Please don't open it. There was only one worn section of the catalog, ragged from the number of times Alex had opened to that page. He was certain if his grandfather put the catalog down, it would fall to his favored section naturally, open to pages of men modeling underwear.

He bit his lip, rolled over in bed, and tried not to cry. His cheeks burned hot with shame.

Alex's cheeks turned pink when he thought about that day. There was a sting of guilt in getting caught with a catalog so revealing, his own personal lust file, even if his grandfather didn't know what he'd found. That, and Alex's own unwillingness to admit who he was. Mostly, he was ashamed of himself knowing he'd never live up to his family's expectations for him.

Even now, thinking about it, he could picture the images in his mind, the ones he'd stared at as a teen again and again, and his thoughts wandered to his unfulfilled needs, the same things he felt guilty for thinking about. He wrapped his hand around himself, stroking and running his fingers along the tip, eyes heavy-lidded as he gave in to his desire. He was slick with water and with need, and he used that, shutting his eyes altogether as he considered lips on his skin, fingers on his body, anything to help him get off. He used one hand to tease at his own nipples, mind pretending someone else was doing the same with his fingers, or perhaps his tongue. Virgin didn't begin to cover how far he'd pushed himself into the closet, but he could picture what sex might feel like, guard down and desperation evident in the way his breath hitched.

Not being out didn't mean he hadn't thought about getting this, hadn't craved and desired the sensual touch. At twenty-two years old, how could he not have at least thought about intimacy? He wanted to know the feeling of having a man on him, what it might be like to taste his lips and hear him breathe. He squeezed a drizzle of conditioner on his hand, sliding a finger into himself as he kept stroking, faster and faster until he was dissolving onto the floor, ashamed of letting himself give in to his feelings. Tears streamed down his face—he was lonely, frustration and need palpable, and he was tired. He was tired physically, from the lack of adequate sleep lately. He was tired emotionally, sick of hiding who he was and being ashamed of what he wanted.

For the first time since he'd been in Omaha, he realized maybe his need to move had less to do with getting away from his past, and more to do with opening himself up to a fresh start, not only in his career aspirations, but perhaps in his other desires too.

But then he realized how foolish the idea of coming out here was. He could tell people here, but eventually word of who he really was would get back to his family. He could see the whole reaction now—his mother spitting her morning coffee out over a social media post someone tagged him in at a pride parade. Coming out wasn't a risk worth taking. He pushed the worries from his mind, choosing instead to focus on the fact that there were caramels on the tray he'd found at his door. He turned his water off without ever bothering to wash his hair or body, drying himself and wrapping the damp towel around his waist.

He didn't bother getting dressed. Instead, he walked through his bedroom to the kitchen and put a caramel into his mouth. The experience was divine. The buttery flavor and lingering saltiness made the caramel richer than he'd anticipated, and he found himself shoving another into his mouth, then picking up the entire plate and settling into the recliner. He couldn't stop his intrusive thoughts, so he gave into them, not the idea of opening up, but to the concerns and anxiety piling on as Christmas approached.

There was no sense in going back home. Not to a family preoccupied with their own problems, a family who would never love him for who he was, a family who he was sure would turn away from him if they knew his secret. There was some sense in eating caramels though. Sense in eating, and sense in hitting the gym, because indulging in this only made sense if he worked out after.

Alex didn't realize he'd eaten the entire plate of caramels until he reached for another one and touched an empty plate instead. He looked down and immediately regretted his mindless overindulgence. There was a special sense of loss in getting to the last bite, a special kind of grief about having eaten the final piece before he could prepare his mouth to fully appreciate the flavor. He glanced toward the tray, the temptation strong to taste the fudge, or to perhaps eat another cookie. But he hadn't intended to finish an entire plate of caramels. Yeah, he *definitely* needed to get to the gym later. For the time being, the sheer joy he'd gotten from the caramels warranted a small act of apology on his part. He sat at his desk and pulled out a piece of paper.

> *Thanks for the Christmas food. It's all great. Or, everything I ate so far. Sorry I yelled at you last night. You were loud and the noise definitely sucked, but I was drunk and a total jerk.*
>
> *Merry Christm—*

The attempt was…awful, to say the least. "Sure, Alex, let's get a fresh start with your insane neighbor by telling him how much he sucks," he muttered to himself.

Thanks for the treats. They were good.

Alex

"God, what are we in, first grade?" Alex ripped the paper and threw the second note in the trash with the first one.

Sorry for yelling at you. The treats were really good. Thanks for bringing them, in spite of how rude I was. I'm sorry I didn't come in for pie, but I wasn't sure coming in for pie in the middle of the night while I was in my bathrobe was a very goo—

"Why is this so hard?" A thank you note should have been simple enough to write. Sure, there was the pressure mounting from knowing the last thing he could afford to do was push away a potential friend. The isolation was weighing on his mind. But he also struggled with the fact that he'd not only made a terrible first impression, but a worse second one. His own frustration at himself left him facing more of a challenge than he'd realized in writing this note. He tore the third letter up, too, thinking long and hard before putting pen to paper again.

Nicholas,

Wow. Those bacon cookies are a surprise. I mean that in a good way. The caramels were great too. I'm looking forward to trying the rest. Sorry for being a jerk last night. I was a little drunk, and you were only trying to have a good time. Thanks for the treats,

Alex

P.S. If you worked The Head and the Heart into your next Christmas playlist, I wouldn't be as mad at the noise.

Alex second-guessed the last part, carefully copying the top half of the note onto a sheet of paper, leaving off the postscript. He was in no position to make a request, even a joking one. He wasn't sure the note itself was perfect, but this one was better than any other attempt he'd made. Plus, what he'd written was remarkably better than anything he'd said to Nicholas in person.

Before he could second-guess himself any more, he picked up the note, folded it in half, and walked to the door, before realizing he was about to deliver it buck naked. "Wow. You really are going for an impression, aren't you?" He shook his head and walked to his room, tugging on clothes and pushing ahead, walking across the hall before he could change his mind.

He thought about knocking, giving Nicholas the note in person. *No, hand-delivery is too much. Awkward.* Then, he thought about doing what Nicholas had done: putting the note at his door, ringing the bell, and running off before Nicholas could see him. Instead, he settled for slipping the paper under the door without so much as a word or a knock. He was a little afraid if they spoke face-to-face, he'd make another grouchy comment and defeat the entire purpose. This way, Nicholas would find the note, but Alex wasn't going to wait around to see his reaction. Instead, he went back to his apartment, focused on how the fudge tasted and considering how much exercise he'd have to do to burn it off.

Alex. His name is Alex. Nicholas couldn't stop thinking about the note, or about the fact that Alex had said something nice to him. He liked the caramels. The past tense he used implied he'd already finished them. Nicholas eyed his counter, looking at the still full glass container.

He considered putting more on a plate, then taking them to Alex to talk, but Alex's slipping the note under the door spoke volumes about whether or not he might want to have a chat, especially since he'd once criticized Nicholas's desperate need to feed people. He walked to the counter and picked up a caramel. Closing his eyes, he lifted it to his lips. As he ate, he tried to think about what someone who had never tasted one would think, what Alex would have experienced tasting it for the first time. He couldn't fully get into his mindset, too used to the taste. It didn't matter. All he could think about was one thing: Alex liked them.

Before he could second-guess himself again, he put another dozen on a plate, covered them in cling wrap, scribbled a quick note, and walked across the hall, setting the treat on the floor.

> *Glad you liked the caramels. Here are a few extras in case you run out.*
>
> *Nicholas*

Chapter Four

Surrender

Nicholas peeked out the bedroom window, sheer curtains allowing the moonlight in. Bright enough to wake him, the eerie blue-white glow shined in a way that could only mean one thing: snow, and a lot of it. He reached for his blanket, wrapping the fabric and the warmth around himself tightly as he stood at the window. For a long while, he watched the snow fall in large, wet flakes, certainly already sticking to the frozen ground. He had been waiting for this since winter began.

At half past four in the morning, Nicholas glanced at his watch before turning his attention fully to the snow. A more reasonable man would have gone back to bed, but Nicholas knew his judgment and reason flew out the window at the first big snowfall. Besides, if he wanted to pull off his plan—the idea that had nagged at the back of his mind as soon as he'd seen the forecast—he'd need to start now.

If he didn't hurry, the store might sell out of the basic supplies. As soon as a few other people had the same idea he had, the necessary items would be gone. He took one last lingering look at the falling snow, and that was enough to spur him into action, no matter how exhausted he should have been. He got dressed and tugged on heavy boots to keep the snow at bay, then drove to the store in silence. Even Christmas music was too much for the soft serenity of snowfall, the gentle flakes sticking to his window.

In the store, he went to the carrots first. They were always the most likely to sell out, but the store was well-stocked, plenty available since no one else was awake to notice the falling snow yet. Sixty carrots, he thought, were perfect for his big idea, and whatever he didn't use would be perfect in a giant pot of soup, enough for his friends and then leftovers for the shelter nearby. He could call to ask if they could take soup. If not, maybe they could use the produce.

He didn't need a written list this time, not the way he did for baking. Now, the list was in his head. All he had to do was find it. Decorative twigs, hot cocoa, flavored coffee creamer—as many as he thought he could reasonably use—each item would make the day more festive and more fun.

"Excuse me," Nicholas said, turning toward a man in a blue vest, focused on stocking a shelf. Despite the early hour, he had a smile on his face. "Do you know if there are any more bags of charcoal?"

"If we 'ave 'em, they'll be outside where we usually keep the grills. Everything's all switched to Christmas stuff right now, but there might be some." He eyed Nicholas skeptically. "What're you using coal for in the middle of winter?" He squinted in disbelief even though Nicholas hadn't answered him yet.

The man was full around the midsection, with a white bushy beard hanging low over his chest. If Nicholas smiled hard enough, he thought perhaps he'd be able to make out a twinkle in the man's eye.

"Just building some snowmen," Nicholas grinned, lifting a bag of carrots from his cart to show the man. "Thanks for your help—" He squinted to make out the name tag. "—Kris. I'll look outside."

"All right, then. Merry Christmas." The man offered a small smile in return.

In the outside garden section of the store, which had been converted into a winter wonderland with inflatable snowmen and reindeer for purchase, he was able to find one last bag of charcoal tucked away in a corner as if it had been forgotten from the summer season. He hoped the bag would have enough for everyone. With one final idea, he pushed the cart through the aisles—all free of shoppers at so early in the morning—running and jumping on it to glide for a few seconds, eyes wide. He felt weightless. No one paid much attention to him: the grown man cart surfing through the nearly empty store. As he reached the aisle he was seeking, he slowed down and piled gloves and scarves and winter hats into his cart, as many as fit into his budget, and headed toward the checkout.

The cashier eyed him, looking at the mounds of supplies piled onto the belt before six in the morning. He was too awake and too cheerful, and his attitude must have thrown her off. "Are you feeding grilled carrots to a small army of frozen children?" she asked, deadpan, but her cheeky smile said she was trying to flirt.

Nicholas, of course, was unruffled as he smiled back sincerely. "How'd you know?" He chuckled softly, trying to brush off her flirtation. "I'm spreading a little Christmas cheer; that's all."

"Wish someone would spread some cheer to me," she mumbled.

"For what it's worth, I hope you have a very Merry Christmas," Nicholas said, swiping his card as she rang the last of the items. He fished in his pocket for a mini candy cane to offer her.

"Thanks." She smiled back at him.

On his way out to the car, he had an extra bounce in his step. There was more snow on the ground now, some falling as he'd gone inside. They'd have plenty to work with.

The sun started to rise on the horizon as he pulled into the parking lot of his apartment. He had precious little time to finish preparing if he wanted to be outside again before anyone left for the day for work or anything else their plans held. He left the carrots, coal, and clothing in the car, setting to work inside brewing coffee and cocoa to fill his largest thermoses.

Back outside, he spread the supplies on the ledge in front of his building, a makeshift sign beside it reading, BUILD A SNOWMAN! A sign wasn't enough, so Nicholas started to work on his own snowman to drive his point home. Not having someone to build a snowman with him made the task harder, but he didn't mind at all. Years of growing up in snowy conditions readied him for this. He heaped a second ball on top of the first one he'd rolled, then another smaller one for the head. He pulled a candy cane from his pocket and sucked on the end as he grabbed coal and carrots to decorate. With all the effort, he barely noticed the cold snap of wind.

"Morning, Nick." The front door squeaked closed as Jade ran up and hugged him from behind, heavy boots crunching in the snow the whole way. "What's up today? Snowmen?"

"Yup. There's a whole heck of a lot of snow, and I thought we'd have fun. Need some coal?" He gestured to the freshly fallen powder, and to his stash of supplies, and then up at the sky as the snow kept falling, darting his tongue out.

She pulled a carrot from the bag, raising an eyebrow. "You really are a strange bird."

"What do you mean?"

"You know. The baking. This," she said, gesturing. "Going to blow your whole inheritance in one Christmas?"

Thankfully, Nicholas knew his spirit endeared most people. Most of them. Alex was the exception. "I'd rather spend the money making people happy than wasting it on something pointless." He shrugged. "And snowmen make everyone happy, don't they?"

"All right. I'll build one," she said, as if she hadn't already planned to join in. "But I'm eating this first." She took a bite from the carrot in her hand.

"Oh no! Not the noses!" Nicholas wailed, reaching out to swat at her hand as he slid off the ledge. "Come on, let's do this." He packed snow into a ball and passed it to her to start rolling, helping her when the base got heavier.

"What are you going to do with all of these hats?"

"I'll gather them up when the snow melts and take them to the shelter, probably." He was hopeful everything would still be needed once their fun was over.

"You're too good for this world, Nick. I don't know how you think of this stuff." She tugged a black beanie down onto her snowman's head.

He shook his head. "You're only saying nice things so I'll invite you for soup later," he said, laughing. Out of the corner of his eye he saw the door swing open again. He would have called out a friendly greeting, but the glimpse of reddish hair—perfectly styled, no less—stopped him in his tracks and made his heart beat in his ears. "Hey, uh...Alex." Alex wasn't dressed for the weather. His slender frame needed more than the light jacket he wore, clearly too cold for the Omaha winter, whether or not there was snow on the ground. He did have a scarf, but he didn't have a hat or gloves. Nicholas kicked himself for not picking any in adult sizes. He couldn't even offer him one. How unprepared did he have to be not to have anything warmer? Anyone nearby, within a few state's radius, should have been mostly prepared for how cold a Nebraska winter would get. He must have been from somewhere else. As the frigid air registered for Alex, Nicholas watched him wrap his arms around himself, shivering.

"Hey."

This was the most they'd spoken face-to-face since Nicholas found out Alex's name. Since Alex had yelled at him for the loud music, really. Nicholas tried to keep his cool when the realization dawned on him. "Want some carrots and coal?" He wasn't sure where they stood, if Alex was mad about their first two introductions, despite the note.

"Whoa, now, you're offering coal? We've only known each other for a whole ten minutes, and you've decided I'm on the naughty list?" Alex tried to glare, but the smile playing on his lips made his gentle ribbing obvious. Nicholas softened, catching the joke once he saw the gleam in Alex's green eyes.

"I don't know. Can you prove you don't belong there?" Nicholas quipped back. He grinned widely, cheeks puffy and flushed in the cold.

"I guess I can't. You're going to have to take my word for it, Nicholas." Alex really *couldn't* prove anything to Nicholas, not when every interaction they'd shared had gone less than stellar, but he got the impression they might be talking about drastically different naughty lists entirely. Alex's eyebrows raised slightly.

"Well, then. You could prove it. We're making snowmen. Or, uh. Snow people." Nicholas tried to shove down the flutter of warmth he got from Alex joking with him. This was a huge leap from Alex standing in his bathrobe grumbling at the noise, now that they were laughing. The tray of treats and the notes they'd exchanged had done wonders, a world of difference for them. Nicholas was happy he'd gone with his gut and put in extra effort instead of leaving an anonymous plate of sweets at Alex's door. *Take that, Jade.*

"Aw, building a snowman sounds fun. But I can't. I've got to get busy if I'm going to get hired someplace before everything gets crazy."

"Employment search? Sounds way less fun than snowmen," Nicholas said.

"I didn't get a lot of response to my online applications, considering the holidays. I figured it couldn't hurt to go and introduce myself face-to-face." He patted the folio tucked under his arm, presumably holding resumes.

"Makes sense. Too bad snow days don't count when you're an adult." Nicholas said. He didn't know why, but he was a little disappointed. "Why not wait until later? I'm pretty sure most places open now will be open this afternoon too." He waggled a carrot toward Alex, holding out hope. Alex started to reach his hand forward, tempted, but then the wind blew, cold against his skin, and he pulled back, stuffing his hands into his pockets.

"Maybe next time." He shrugged. "Sorry. I have to go. Have fun." Alex turned away, clearly trying to hide from the cold wind as he tugged his scarf over his nose. *Oh well.*

"Hey! Help me out here, Alex!"

It took Alex a second to realize Mike was talking to him. He was distracted by the sunlight, the sound of waves, and the way Mike's biceps looked, exposed in his bright-yellow tank top. "Help with what?"

"Lifting this! I can't get the ball on there."

"Really? You missing the gym lately or are you weak as hell?" Alex taunted, but he pushed off his towel and headed toward Mike.

"Shut up and help me," Mike said. Even with both of them, the sand was too dry, crumbling before Mike could ever live his dream of building a "sandman," as he'd called it. Whatever, the ocean awaited them, and by the time Alex's feet hit the water, he'd forgotten all about it.

The cold wasn't the only thing Alex tried to hide from. With all of the reasons he'd left Los Angeles, the last thing he needed was to befriend a tall, attractive, cheerful man who couldn't stop popping into his life at the most inconvenient times. Friendship hadn't gone well for him in the past, and this time was no different.

He had work to get done. He didn't have time for this kind of snow horseplay.

Nicholas could see the wheels turning in Jade's mind as she looked between him and the back of Alex's head and scooped up a handful of snow, packing it tightly together. "J, no!" he yelled. Too late. Years of softball left Jade with deadly accuracy, and before Nicholas could warn Alex to watch out, the snow slopped against the back of his head, sliding down to land coolly at the nape of his neck.

"What the heck did you do that for?" Alex asked, whipping around. Jade had already ducked behind a snowman, leaving Nicholas as the only real culprit within his line of sight. Everyone else was fully engrossed in snowman and igloo building of their own, or walking to get somewhere. Nicholas, on the other hand, stood there awkwardly, a cup of cocoa in his hand.

Alex reached behind his head, brushing the snow from his hair. "You got some kind of a problem?"

"I am *so* sorry," Nicholas said. He didn't want to throw his best friend under the bus, but he also didn't want to take the fall. Instead, he tried to patch things up by shoving the cocoa toward Alex. "I'm sorry. Have some cocoa? I've got lids! You can take it with you."

"Seriously?" Alex asked, eyebrows raised. "You really think I can go try to get a job when my hair is an absolute mess, and I've got snow running down my back?" He snorted and narrowed his eyes, throwing his folio on the ground. "Nah. Job hunting is going to have to wait." Reaching his bare hand toward the snow on the ledge beside him, he crushed snow together, oblivious to the cold as he out for revenge. "I can't believe you'd throw a snowball at me just because I won't join your weird snowman cult," he said. "Hey, you know what they say about karma?"

Nicholas should have seen the fight coming, because Alex hadn't exactly hidden his revenge, and yet he stood there with a shocked expression, rather than moving away. Alex threw the snowball across the distance between them, Nicholas's expression shifting from shock to utter disbelief as it came too close to dodge. The wad of snow hit Nicholas squarely in the chest as cocoa sloshed out of the cup and onto the snow at his feet.

"I didn't do it!" Nicholas confessed, nestling the cup in the snow. He made his own snowball and hurled the snow, hitting Alex in the shoulder.

"Yeah? You just threw another one. How the heck am I supposed to believe you didn't throw the other one?" He pursed his lips and threw another one, but Nicholas dodged it, barely whizzing past his ear. "Who did, if you didn't?"

"Me!" Jade yelled from behind a snowman. Without looking, she threw another one, and it splattered across Alex's cheek, wet and cold and heavy. He looked at her with narrowed eyes, ready to retaliate with the snowball already in his hand.

"Looks like you owe your friend a huge apology," Alex said, looking between the two of them.

"Yeah!" Nicholas added.

"You want to know why? I'm blaming him because I can." He smiled now, throwing the snowball at Nicholas instead of Jade while the element of surprise was on his side. For someone who had every right to be furious, he was smiling, and Nicholas wasn't too worried.

"Why are you blaming me?" Nicholas asked, but it didn't matter. "Fine. I'll get her, then."

Snowball fights were more exhausting than Alex anticipated. He'd never been in one before, and within minutes, he was out of breath. The activity wasn't the issue—he was in good shape. But he wasn't used to breathing in the cold air as he leaped through heavy snow and threw it at Nicholas and his friend. No matter how many snowballs he threw, Nicholas and his friend never seemed to tire, throwing them right back, both at him and at each other.

Nicholas kept looking away from Alex for a second too long, and finally, Alex used the window of opportunity to hit him with another snowball, right in the hip. Nicholas cracked up, clutching his hip as if dying in battle and falling back onto the snow with a huff. Snow puffed up around him in a soft, feathery, sparkling dust.

Alex ran to him and swept an armful of snow from the ground, dropping it onto Nicholas unceremoniously before flopping down to the ground beside him. "You cold yet? Ready to surrender to my superior snowball skills?" He grinned.

"Me? Cold? Never. Bet you are. You're doing this bare-handed?" He quirked an eyebrow and cocked his head to one side.

For the first time in the whole fight, Alex realized how cold and stiff his hands actually were. Adrenaline had kept him from realizing at first, and he placed a hand on Nicholas's neck. "I don't know. Am I?"

Nicholas flinched, putting a gloved hand on Alex's bare one. "Jeez. Yeah, you're a popsicle!" He pulled Alex's hand off him and took his own gloves off with his teeth, grasping Alex's hands in his and trying to warm them up. "You should take my gloves."

"Then you'll be cold. Sounds like a never-ending cycle. You going to take her gloves next, and then she'll have to grab gloves from someone else, and...?"

"Nah, I have another pair," Nicholas said. "Take them. You clearly need them more than I do." He rubbed his hand over Alex's, and Alex didn't pull away. Nicholas's hands were warm, and he was frozen. "May I?" Nicholas asked, lifting Alex's hands higher and pulling them closer to his lips.

"May you what?"

"Here," Nicholas said. He blew warm air onto them.

Alex resisted the urge to jerk away, a little embarrassed at how much he liked the sensation. The friction and breath helped his hands, certainly, but there was a flurry of warmth tingling through other parts of him too.

"Your current wardrobe isn't going to cut it if you're going to be here a while."

"Thanks for the advice," Alex said, watching the way Nicholas was tending to his hands, switching between blowing hot breath and rubbing his hands together over Alex's. Alex was certain his shortness of breath was no longer from the cold air or the activity, but from being in close proximity to Nicholas like this. He was overwhelmed.

"Where are you from, anyway?"

"Los Angeles."

Nicholas wiggled Alex's fingers, rubbing them individually and moving them back and forth.

"What are you doing?" Alex asked him.

"Making sure you don't have frostbite." His eyes flicked up to meet Alex's, his tone serious. "You're a long way from home, then. You really should take these gloves.

At least borrow them until you get some, you know? It isn't like you don't know where I live, so you can return them." He twined Alex's fingers together and cupped them with his hands again.

Alex liked that. He liked the sensation and the warmth, and he liked having Nicholas's hands on his own, soft against his without gloves between them. He hated the idea that he wanted more, wanted for Nicholas to keep touching his hands like that. Even then, he looked up and saw Nicholas looking back at him, smiling softly. Alex realized what he was letting happen, the closeness they were sharing, and his eyes went wide as panic rose in his throat. The touch wasn't the issue as much as the fact that he wanted more, how he was tempted to go get frostbite if Nicholas would keep taking care of him. That, his desire for more, he didn't like.

> *"Come on, get in here, the water's fine!" Alex laughed, grabbing Mike's hand and tugging him toward the water. "Wimp."*
>
> *Mike jerked his hand away. "Fine. I'll get in. If you don't try to hold my hand again." He winked at Alex, but the wink only fueled Alex's conflicting feelings.*
>
> *"Wasn't trying to hold your hand, jackass. Trust me."*
>
> *"It's a joke, man. You don't have to get defensive," Mike said. And then he was splashing through the waves, running far past where Alex stood.*

"I-I gotta go. I...bye." Alex pushed himself off the ground and rushed into the building, away from job applications he'd hoped to follow up on, but mostly away from Nicholas. Behind him, he could hear Nicholas encouraging him to wait a second, apologizing, and other words he couldn't make out in his haste.

Alex ignored him and let the door close between himself and the outside world, then raced up the stairs to his floor, feet pounding as his heart beat wildly in his chest. As the door to his apartment closed behind him, he leaned against the wall, resting his cold hands on his knees. Tears stung his eyes. He felt like an idiot.

His life was on repeat. He was attracted to a guy and his inner monologue was telling him "Nicholas can't feel the same; he can't; this is stupid." He knew most of his thought process was irrational, and either way didn't mean anything. They barely knew each other! But he couldn't control his inner fear, and he couldn't let himself get attached to someone here, especially not a stranger like Nicholas. If he did, things would go out of control like they did in LA, with Alex hurt and trying to pick up the pieces from his own drama and life, trying to keep his secrets and juggling everything as the world crashed down on him. He wasn't meant for personal relationships—friendships or otherwise—especially because he barely knew Nicholas in the first place. He was stupid to get wrapped up in the snowball fight, in the easy tangles of new friendships. Not when Alex was...Alex. Awkward, uneasy Alex.

"Alex? Hey, can we talk for a second?" Nicholas was knocking on the door, and Alex didn't want to answer. After a moment, the knocking stopped, and he realized he at least owed Nicholas some kind of explanation so he opened the door.

"Hi."

"Hi," Nicholas said. After Alex didn't say anything else, he added, "I'm sorry. I wasn't trying to be pushy about the gloves."

"It's okay."

"One time a friend of mine from high school got frostbite, and she ended up losing her pinky. I worry, is all."

"I appreciate your concern." Alex couldn't meet his gaze, and he felt guilty as a result. "Listen, Nicholas, you're...you're really nice. I just..." He paused, taking a slow, shaky breath. "I can't."

"Can't what?"

"I don't know," Alex said, looking down and shifting his weight between his feet. "I should probably go get cleaned up and check up on my applications."

"Okay. In that case, you probably need this. You left it in the snow," he said, handing Alex's folio toward him. "I'll see you around, Alex. Let me know if you ever decide if you...um...can."

Nicholas wasn't sure why he kept trying with Alex. He'd been so thrown off by him. First, an insistence he hated peppermint, then an apparent hatred toward all things Christmas, judging by his door and general disposition. Alex had even yelled at him once, but in Alex's defense, Nicholas had been loud. He understood. All of that made sense to him. What didn't make sense was the whiplash of Alex now: the nice note under his door, his involvement when he could have left the situation after Jade instigated the snowball fight. He'd dived across the snow to put his hands on Nicholas's face. Nicholas couldn't help but wonder what he'd done to scare him off, what it was that Alex...couldn't.

Maybe he'd gone too far in taking Alex's hand, but Alex had let him, had stayed and allowed Nicholas to warm him up. Nicholas couldn't be sure what part of what he'd done was too far, though, and he kicked himself for doing whatever sent Alex running. Maybe Alex could tell he was gay—he didn't make his sexuality a secret—and was uncomfortable with that. Nicholas hadn't been hitting on him, and he would've done the same thing for Jade. He was trying to be nice. But Alex didn't necessarily know he was only being kind.

He didn't know Alex well enough to know how to read him, to know if somehow Alex had interpreted what they'd done as more than friendly banter, even if Nicholas hadn't intended anything more. Then again, he couldn't be certain he wasn't flirting with Alex. In a way, he was. There had been other ways to keep Alex's hands warm. He could have insisted on the gloves, could have at least made him hold the cocoa. Instead, he'd gone straight for taking his hands and breathing on them. So yeah, Nicholas thought. He had flirted a little. But Alex touched him first, he reminded himself. Even then, he couldn't blame Alex for running, whether or not he understood why. He shook his head and walked back outside into the cold.

Alex heard Nicholas's footsteps fade down the hallway. Running after him crossed his mind, but trying to explain how making new friends meant confronting his own thoughts and feelings...thoughts and feelings Alex wasn't ready to face. Letting a new friend into his life in even the smallest capacity was a recipe for disaster.

He needed to get ready to go, to track down a job. At this point, he'd settle for a temporary one until he could get a more suitable position. He could apply at a coffeeshop, maybe, if he couldn't find a tech-specific job yet, but he couldn't bring himself to do that either. Instead, he took a page from his mother's playbook—going to his room and lying down, pulling the covers over his head. His mind focused on the year before, the last time he'd let someone into his life at all. Mike was, for all intents and purposes, his *best* friend. They'd met in school in the fall of freshman year, and when they did, Alex was so certain they'd be lifelong friends, the kind who had weekend barbecues together, telling everyone stories about the old times back in college, the fun and trouble they'd gotten into. They had connected so quickly, spending most of their free time together, going on spring break twice. The first time, they'd had to share a bed thanks to a hotel mixup that left them in the wrong building, away from friends, and in the last available room they had. Sharing a room wasn't unusual, since half the time, Mike said he could sleep in his dorm instead of commuting home before his eight o'clock class the next morning, but the bed sharing was an experience.

They had so much in common. It all felt natural. Misreading Mike's kindness as more, as flirtation, was far too easy. Alex didn't realize, until too late, that Mike wasn't flirting, but Alex had certainly thought he was, at the time. Heck, Mike had once joked if they weren't married by the time they were in grad school, they should "do it for the taxes, man." Alex kicked himself for thinking the words meant anything more than a joke. Their friendship had crumbled for...obvious reasons, he realized. When Alex graduated after the fall semester during their senior year, five months before his peers, he shut himself off completely.

The last thing Alex wanted now was a friend, someone he might develop feelings for. If Nicholas was anything like Mike, feelings were likely inevitable, and he hated it. If he found one friendship gone wrong was isolating in LA, he could only imagine how he would feel to lose people now, when he had no one else. Trying to make a friend could only lead to rejection, or unrequited love, or any number of other awful outcomes. None of those were pleasant thoughts, not when he'd come so far to escape the ache that came with unreciprocated interest. Friendship? Being around people? Not worth the risk.

Or, maybe the effort was worth the risk if Alex thought he could be Nicholas's friend without ever being attracted to him. If there was a way he could confirm he'd only ever want to be his friend, he might have gone for it. Lying under the covers in his bed, he let his mind go there. He let himself accept the fact that he was completely, definitively, entirely attracted to Nicholas, from his tall frame decked out in candy-cane-striped sweaters, to the weird way nothing seemed to ever bring him down. His draw to Nicholas started at his personality—how could anyone resist someone so cheerful?—but he admitted his attraction to Nicholas was physical too.

Alex was interested in him. But even if Alex knew he'd never push for more than friendship—Nicholas probably wouldn't be interested in the first place—it was for that reason, that interest, that Alex could never, ever let himself be Nicholas's friend.

Chapter Five

Breaking a Sweat

"Is everything okay?" Jade asked. She didn't let Nicholas get all the way outside before starting in on the questions. Alex had gone from touching Nicholas to running inside in a matter of seconds, so fast Nicholas practically got whiplash, and he knew she wanted answers as much as Nicholas did. Maybe more.

"I don't know. All he said was 'I can't.'"

"Can't what?"

"I don't know." Nicholas slumped his shoulders as Jade passed him an almost-empty thermos of coffee. His posture and demeanor made him look so much smaller than he was. He looked out at the army of snowmen everyone had been building, perking up knowing he'd at least spread *some* cheer, even if he was otherwise completely disheartened.

Jade took the coffee and sipped it, thinking aloud. "Don't stress. He'll come around, and if he doesn't, what did you actually know about him? He's probably horrible." She snorted.

"He isn't," Nicholas said. As soon as he'd said the words, he realized he had nothing to back it up with. He didn't actually know Alex well enough to defend him to Jade. "I know he hates peppermint. Or at least, he hates peppermint bark. Or he likes it and told me he doesn't. I'm not really sure which."

"Okay. Sounds like a lot to go on right there. You either know or don't know. Helpful, Nick."

"I think he might have said he didn't so I wouldn't feel guilty about taking the last box at the store. He sort of got touchy about it." Nicholas thought. "He doesn't like people playing Christmas music in the middle of the night, but I can't really blame him for that."

"So *that's* who the tray was for? You could've told me before I pelted him with a snowball," Jade quipped. She ate another carrot.

"If you eat all of those, there won't be any for soup later. You're coming for soup tonight, by the way. I'm not taking no for an answer." He sighed. "As if you didn't know, anyway. You could tell by looking at him he's who I gave the treats to, Ms. So-Sure-About-My-Type. And even if I *had* told you, you probably only would've pelted him harder."

"You know me too well sometimes." She nudged his shoulder. "Doesn't matter. He's into you. And he'll come around."

"He's not into me." Interested people don't yell at people they like in the middle of the night and don't run at the first chance they have to connect. Interested people definitely don't end conversations with a cryptic statement about how they "can't," whatever the heck he meant.

"He held your hand after knowing you for all of twenty minutes, Nick."

"Yeah, and he ran off right after. He's not into me."

"Yeah, okay." Her sarcasm was palpable.

"Trust me, J. He couldn't have made it clearer if he tried." Nicholas grabbed the unused snowman supplies, cleaning up the mess on the ledge. "Technically, by the way, I held *his* hands. Doesn't matter. I'll see you at dinner tonight. Seven. Bring V." He leaned in and kissed her cheek, arms too full for a hug.

"Can't do tonight. Tomorrow? Also, she's going to tell you the same thing I did. He likes you. And if he doesn't, that's his loss."

Nicholas didn't justify her certainty with a response. Instead, he answered, "Tomorrow," and tried to shut out the rest.

Alex peeled himself out of bed. Lying around moping wasn't going to get him anywhere. It hadn't for his mother, and he was really no different. Heaving a sigh, he stood and walked to the mirror. He could see the changes in his body, the protective layer of fat from the first part of an Omaha winter and the tray of baked goods he'd been demolishing. That, or he could have been imagining things. Truth be told, he'd gotten too skinny the past year from stress, but he didn't think toning could hurt. If nothing else, the endorphins might help his mood.

He tugged on his favorite workout shorts and a tank top, thankful the apartment had a gym he could use without going outside. Halfway down, in the elevator, he realized the irony of taking an elevator instead of the stairs when his plan was to work out. *Too late.* As he stepped off, putting his earbuds in and turning the volume up, he was happy with his decision. "Let's go," he whispered to himself, and he opened the gym, ready to get in a better frame of mind.

Empty and quiet, Alex had the right idea to go to the gym when he did. No one to interrupt, no one to watch him, no one to try to spark conversation when he was here to get drenched in sweat. The apartment gym was well-stocked with equipment, so anything he wanted to do, he could. Weights, yoga, running—it featured the basics he needed. Mostly, he planned to run.

In LA, running had been a good way to clear his mind. He hadn't lived too horribly far from a beach, so when he really needed to get out of his head for a little bit, Malibu Surfrider Beach had been his preferred go-to spot so he could go surfing and then go for a run. Here, running on a beach wasn't an option. Heck, being outside wasn't an option in the current weather, not when the snow hadn't melted from the day before.

He tried not to think about that part.

Alex didn't mind running inside though. Running was less about the scenery and more about the burn in his lungs and the way his legs could ache in the best ways after a good workout. Starting slow, he warmed up with a low-incline, brisk walk. The treadmill was nicer than his mom's back home, which he rarely used, and he let it carry him on a run with adjusting inclines and speeds and times, forcing him to keep up when he hadn't worked out since before he moved.

He held his own, tuning out and listening to the music thrumming in his ears, letting his feet fall into rhythm with the beat. He let his mind wander as he did, thinking about home and running there, thinking about his mom and how he was forcing himself to face his problems differently, then thinking about Nicholas.

Would being his friend really be so bad? Alex wasn't so ridiculous to think he'd hit on every man he was attracted to, nor did he think he'd hit on every friend he made. He was convinced his fear of being Nicholas's friend came from past issues, mistakes he wouldn't let himself make again. They could be platonic friends. Alex wasn't in a position to turn friendship away. As long as he kept his head on straight, didn't make any sort of weird moves, he wanted to try to be Nicholas's friend. He didn't have another choice. Nicholas was genuinely nice—too nice to resist befriending.

Mostly, Alex let himself get lost in his thoughts, and in the burn in his calves as he ran, not realizing he had company until he saw movement in the corner of his eye. He was startled enough that he almost fell off the treadmill, but he steadied himself, regaining his balance and his rhythm. There was an unspoken gym rule not to stare at people on the nearby machines, but with the large, floor-to-ceiling mirrors in front of them, he couldn't miss how Nicholas had picked the machine right next to him. In a room with three treadmills and plenty of other machines to work on, Nicholas had opted for the one beside him, the one where—if they extended their arms—they'd be touching.

"Hey," Nicholas said.

Alex tapped his ear, pointing at his earbud, and kept running, giving a small wave. Now that he'd settled on friendship, they'd have to talk eventually, but Alex wasn't sure he was ready yet. When he thought about it, he'd thought about friendship on his schedule, at his pace, not friendship barging in while he was trying to work out. Nicholas grinned, glancing at him and then staring him down in the mirror. Alex met his eyes just as easily, blushing and looking away. *Just friends. Don't look at him like that.* Alex had had dozens of friendships with guys in his life and only one resulting in a crash-and-burn ending from unrequited attraction. He'd even had a couple since Mike. He could do this. Couldn't he? Despite the program he'd planned on the treadmill, he was flustered in a way that had nothing to do with incline or speed. He lowered the intensity.

Nicholas, on the other hand, cranked his up, going a little faster. *A challenge.* Alex couldn't resist. Pressing the speed button, he kept breathing as steadily as he could as he let the machine push him harder, let his feet pound against the belt a little heavier. Nicholas took his intensity as the challenge Alex intended it to be and nudged his setting to a harder one. Through the mirror, Alex could see the beads of sweat forming on his forehead, the flush on his cheeks. But Alex couldn't let him win, not like so easily, in this unspoken race of theirs. He pushed the button again. A little faster. A little harder.

Nicholas smirked and shook his head a little, earbuds in as he scrolled through his phone and selected a new song to listen to. He raised an eyebrow and went to full speed, sweat soaking through his shirt. Alex couldn't tear his eyes away from Nicholas in the mirror, but at least the staring was mutual. He hoped Nicholas saw his gaze as part of the challenge and not attraction. He didn't want to have to explain. Alex pressed ahead, full speed, because movement was a good way to keep his mind off of how badly he wanted to talk to Nicholas. If they were running fast—so hard he could barely breathe, let alone speak—he wouldn't have to say what he didn't think he could say yet. So, he didn't say anything. He kept running, and he kept watching Nicholas. Nicholas, and the way sweat prickled on his collarbone, the way it beaded up and slipped down his neck, and how it disappeared under his tank top.

Nicholas, and the way his muscles worked, not only in his legs, but in his arms, his bicep definition apparent as he ran, arms bent, kept near his sides. Nicholas stared back, a small smile, trying to maintain his composure as much as Alex had. Alex's lungs burned with the effort.

Alex didn't stop until the cramp in his side hit him like lightning. He slammed his finger on the stop button, letting the dying whir of the belt slide him back until he planted his feet on the floor, grasping his ribcage. "You win."

Nicholas smirked, dialed down his speed, and pointed to his headphones. "Can't hear you."

Alex was certain Nicholas could hear him, but he wasn't arguing. *He's giving you a free pass. If he can't hear you concede, you're still on even ground.* Alex would take what he could get. As he lifted his shirt and wiped the sweat from his forehead, struggling to catch his breath and get rid of the pain in his side, Nicholas stopped his treadmill altogether.

Pulling his earbuds out, Alex said, "Hey," properly this time.

"Hey," Nicholas answered. Alex wanted to say something, wanted to say anything, but he was struggling to talk at all, gripping his ribcage and rubbing his side.

"Cramp?"

Alex nodded.

"Sorry," Nicholas said meekly.

"Don't be. Was a good challenge," Alex squeaked out between breaths. He composed himself, breathing in and standing a little straighter. "I swear I'm not usually this out of shape. It's just, some guy left a whole bunch of baked goods in front of my door, and—" He inhaled sharply. "—it'd be rude not to eat them."

"I get it. The holidays are made for indulging." Nicholas smiled genuinely.

"Yeah. Hey, about the other day—"

Before Alex could fully prepare what he wanted to say, before he could get the words out, the door swung open. A guy, boombox in his arm already blaring music, stepped inside. Alex tried to raise his voice and talk over the sound.

"I'm sorry. For running away, I mean."

"It's okay!" Nicholas said, a little louder, nearly shouting. He turned to the guy, asking, "Do you mind?"

The guy shrugged, weights in hand. Nicholas sighed. Alex didn't have to be able to hear him to hear that. "Want to talk outside?"

"What?" The room was too small for the noise level, and Alex couldn't handle it. Walking over, he reached out and flipped the switch, killing the guy's music completely. "What were you saying?"

"I was asking if you wanted to talk in the hall," Nicholas clarified.

"Sure," Alex answered, glancing at the guy who was glaring at him. If looks could kill...well, he didn't want to think about it. He clicked the music back on and walked out the door, ducking under Nicholas's outstretched arm as he held the door for Alex. "The nerve of some people, playing extra-loud music like other people don't live in this building." He smirked, trying to make it clear he was only joking.

"Oh gosh, right? So self-absorbed. Could've been worse though. He could've been blaring Christmas music and trying to sing along badly."

"That's true," Alex said, tapping his lips with his forefinger and smiling. "Can I ask you something?"

"You just did."

"What?" Alex asked, then shook his head. "Oh, you're one of *those* people. Fine. I'm *going* to ask you a question and then you can decide if you want to answer."

"Shoot."

"Can I take you up on your glove offer? I haven't been to the store yet, but I'm in that Catch-22 where it's too cold to go to the store without gloves, but I can't get gloves if I don't go." Alex was afraid maybe asking was overstepping, especially since he'd run away the last time they'd talked, but Nicholas smiled.

"Sure. I'll bring them by a little later? I should probably shower first." He lifted an armpit and sniffed, then pulled a dramatic face, scrunched nose and all.

"Yeah, me too. So I'll see you around, then?"

"Yeah. I'll see you around."

"Oh, and Nicholas? Thanks."

"Anytime."

"What if he's straight?" Veronica asked. The question was completely valid.

"First of all, I don't think that's the issue. Secondly, if he is, so what? Is there some sort of rule we couldn't hang out?" Nicholas asked. There wasn't any sort of rule book for this. "It doesn't really matter to me either way."

"Yes, I know it doesn't matter to you. But the thing is, it might matter to him," Veronica said. She slurped her soup, punctuating the thought.

"I don't think so," Jade clarified. "I think you have to give him some time. I mean, you said he was nice after the gym."

"Yeah, but he needed a favor," Veronica said. "And he didn't answer the door."

"We both said we were going to go shower," Nicholas protested. "He might not have heard me. I don't think he's the kind of guy who can swallow his pride enough to be nice enough solely to get a favor. I think he genuinely wanted to be nice."

"I still think he's struggling with something we don't know about," Jade interjected. "Y'all are a bunch of cynics. Even you, Nick, no matter how full you keep your glass." She turned to Veronica. "Did he tell you about the time Alex held hands with him?"

Nicholas groaned and leaned back in his seat. "That is *not* what happened. I held his hands only to warm them up. And he ran away immediately after, so I don't think you can count that as a point in your favor, J."

"I think I can," Jade said. "Either way, I wouldn't write him off yet. Whether or not he's straight, whether or not you're pursuing friendship or whatever else with the dude, don't write him off yet. Are you inviting him to your party?"

"I don't think he'll come," Nicholas explained.

"You don't know that."

"He didn't answer the door for the gloves and coat," Nicholas reminded her, in spite of how he'd just been defending the opposite position to Veronica. They had his head all tangled, his brain confused on what he thought the situation was, and on what he *wanted* it to be.

"Invite him."

"Why?"

"Because if you don't, I will, and it'll be better coming from you since he likes you."

"Does not," Nicholas snorted. Veronica stayed silent, slurping her soup and watching them, eyes going back and forth like watching a tennis match.

"Children," she finally said. "Nicholas, invite him. Jade, don't be bossy, sweetheart." She lifted her bowl to her lips, draining the broth, and pushed her chair away from the table. "I need a drink stronger than wine if I have to keep listening to this."

"Fine. I'll invite him," Nicholas said. "You'll see I'm right when he doesn't show up." For once in his life, Nicholas didn't want to be right.

Chapter Six

One Lone Snowman

Pie plate in hand, Alex looked outside his window at the army of snowmen he hadn't stuck around to help build. He hadn't bothered to cut a slice, instead, eating straight out of the pan. Now, it was half empty, or what someone who wasn't as lonely as he was might have considered half full.

Frustration and sadness were eating at him again. Mostly, he blamed his mood swing on how he'd been a complete and total coward when Nicholas had stopped by with the coat and gloves. He'd heard the knock but was too scared he was pressing his luck after their good conversation at the gym. Instead of opening the door and thanking him face-to-face, he kept washing dishes, thinking "I'll go in a second" and silently hoping Nicholas would stop knocking before he dried his hands. He found a heavy coat, scarf, and gloves hanging on the doorknob when he dared to open the door an hour later, and a note pinned to the clothes.

> *Knocked but you were probably showering. Use them as long as you need... They're an extra set. Trust me, when you get used to Omaha winters, you'll have two sets too. I'm sure.*

P.S. I have some caramels left if you need some more. Just knock!

Nicholas

How could someone that nice be real? He hadn't ruled out that Nicholas was some kind of mythical being, like Santa Claus or an elf. If he was, Alex would definitely be getting coal this year. He was disappointed in himself for not answering. So, he stuffed his frustration down with as much pie as he could, fully aware he'd need to go back to the gym soon. He knew he wasn't handling things in a healthy way, but that didn't mean it didn't make him feel better.

In addition to being impossibly nice, Nicholas was a very skilled baker. Alex sulked away from the window, away from the army of snowmen facing his side of the building. Placing the pie on the counter, he looked at it carefully, then rinsed his fork to stop himself from having another bite.

No matter how much he knew looking would only send him into a spiral of self-wallowing, he sank into his chair and scrolled through his Instagram feed. He hadn't updated his own in months, but looking through the app was a guilty displeasure. The pictures were filled with happy, smiling faces of friends back in LA, all enjoying the holidays with their closest friends and families—all of the things Alex didn't have here. He wouldn't have let himself have it back home, either.

He'd been isolated from his family for a while. His mother's depression wasn't the only factor there. The distance between himself and his family was apparent in the way his grandfather said, "New marriage laws? What a bunch of special snowflakes," when watching the news, or the way his grandmother answered with, "Yeah, the LGBLMNOP group has to think they get their own set of rules." He couldn't bring himself to get closer to them. He was too scared to make too many new close friends, either—anything beyond surface friendships—for fear he might ruin them. His year since he'd graduated, a few shallow friendships aside, had been isolating and exhausting, a blur of work, sleep, and hiding in his room to avoid human contact.

You'd have a friend here if you put in the effort, Alex thought, but shortly afterward, his brain ventured back into dark territory where he started to panic again, worrying that no, he couldn't, because he'd only manage to mess everything up again.

He sat in his chair, wrestling with his concern. There was no right answer here. He didn't want to go through his whole life avoiding friendships altogether because of one bad interaction, especially because talking to Nicholas had been really nice. But, he was scared to start fresh here. If being authentic led to problems, if he scared Nicholas away by coming out to him at some point, by telling him the truth about who he was, he'd have to uproot and move to a new place. Not that he'd actually move again over *this,* but it would have been preferable to the awkwardness of living across the hall from Nicholas for the next couple of years. In the end, he felt frustrated with himself. He could sense his overreactive mind wanting to make him believe he could never manage to find peace about what happened before, make him think everyone would avoid him as soon as they found out he was gay. He hadn't trusted many people with the truth, and the one he did confide in hated him.

He didn't want to prove himself right. He would make friends here, if it was the last thing he did, even if he made a fool of himself trying. He sighed and stood up, pulling on the coat Nicholas loaned him. His own warmest jacket wasn't nearly warm enough, considering how cold winters got in Omaha compared to back home, and thin fabric gloves were not right for what he wanted to do either. Nicholas's coat smelled nice, and Alex wasn't surprised in the slightest by the scent of cinnamon and cloves, warming in and of itself.

His refrigerator was mostly bare, but he did have baby carrots. They'd have to work. When he got outside, the cold air stung his face. The frigid chill still managed cut through the protective layers of clothing more than he'd expected. He was thankful for the gloves and coat. Now wasn't the time to focus on whether or not he should have brought the scarf too. Instead, he chose to focus on figuring out exactly where he was going to do this, to make his plan work.

Alex walked around the side of the building to the back, counting windows as he did to try to find the right place. Once he did, he began rolling, making a large snowball, then another. He tried to figure out how to lift the midsection of his snowman on top of the base. Building a snowman wasn't quite like in the movies, and his first two attempts crumbled. By the third, he gave up, cheeks raw from the cold, so he hoisted the remains onto the lower section, trying to shape a body as best as he could. His final creation wasn't perfect or pretty, but it would work.

He formed a tiny, misshapen head in his hands. The sphere wasn't a sphere so much as a lumpy...something, not neat and clean like the army of snowmen in front of the building, but that was the price he paid for building one alone instead of trying with everyone else. For his first-ever snowman, it didn't look half bad. For a long while—or what was probably seconds but felt longer in the cold—he stood and admired what he'd made. But then he remembered why he was doing this in the first place. He needed to finish. Fishing a baby carrot from his pocket, he pushed it carefully into the snowman's head, trying to secure the nose without destroying what he'd made. He didn't have any coal, but he improvised, using two pebbles he'd found near the doorway, uncovered by snow that had drifted after falling. They didn't match, but they looked like eyes all the same.

Alex didn't have a chance at finding decent sticks, only getting one long craggy one. He stuck it in the side of the snowman as if the snowman were waving, then draped a sign around his neck, packing snow over the twine to keep it in place. He hoped he'd counted the windows correctly so the snowman would be near enough to Nicholas's apartment for him to see. As he walked away and headed inside, he took one last glance at the snowman he'd left there. In large black permanent-marker letters, he could see the words boldly.

THANK YOU

Alex warmed his hands inside the entryway, thankful they weren't nearly as cold as they'd been earlier. Nicholas's gloves had helped. He couldn't keep them forever, and his raw, red, wind-whipped face said Nicholas had been right about a scarf being essential. He needed to get himself warmer clothing for sure.

First, mail. The tiny metal door to his mailbox was jammed, a struggle to open, and he quickly realized it had gotten caught on some sort of card or note stuffed in there, likely not by the mailman. He jiggled the door, tugging until it came free and a bright yellow paper drifted to the floor. He barely caught it.

Holiday Party

Apartment 14B

December 9, 8:00 p.m.

Bring your favorite cookies

and wear your ugliest sweater

Below the typed print and bold Christmas graphics, there was a quick scrawl written in pen.

Sorry for the late notice. I hope you'll come anyway. There's going to be a whole group, so no pressure to hang out with me specifically. I might even invite Mr. Boombox. ;)

Nicholas

Alex cringed at the part about not hanging out with him specifically. Did he come off that harsh sometimes? Yeah, he did. Either way, Nicholas was inviting him to a party. He was on the precipice, deciding between loneliness and new connections, the comfort of solid ground and the free fall of emotions jumping in could bring. He didn't know which would be the best choice.

"Hey, you're Nicholas's new friend, right?" A voice came from behind him, one he couldn't place, and he turned to see the girl Nicholas claimed threw the snowball.

"No. I mean, yeah. Kind of." Alex stumbled over his words. Friends? Not really. Not yet. Acquaintances until Alex inevitably blew it? Definitely. "We've talked a few times." He decided on. "I don't know." He didn't know why he was getting into this here, why he was awkwardly scratching the back of his neck and trying to define acquaintanceship with a stranger. Besides, his awkwardness was no one's business but his own. A simple yes or no would have sufficed. Alex couldn't drop it there, so he was left retreating from the ledge again, thinking maybe a party was a terrible idea after all.

He could tell by her smile that she knew he wanted to exit the conversation. Clearly, she wasn't letting him off the hook. "You're going to the party, though, right?" He folded his invitation up quickly in hopes of hiding the personal note at the bottom.

"I don't know. I think I, uh... I think I have...a thing? Like a work thing." He stumbled and stuttered, lying through his teeth.

"I thought you said you hadn't found work yet. Isn't that why Nicholas took your folder thing to you this morning?" She raised an eyebrow, clearly calling him out on his lie.

"Oh. Right. Well, I'll see what I can do," he said, shrugging and turning back to collect the rest of his mail. "I'll see you around," he said, without turning to look at her.

"See you at the party," she corrected, and he could hear her fiddling with her mailbox.

A part of Alex desperately wanted to go, but the other part wanted to avoid the party in the interest of self-preservation. He didn't even own an ugly sweater. He considered it, though, stuffing the mail into the inner pocket of Nicholas's coat. He took two steps forward toward the stairs leading to his apartment, then turned back and walked to his car again. He needed to buy his own coat, his own gloves. If he happened to stumble on an ugly sweater while he was there, maybe he'd decide to actually attend.

Nicholas stirred the potpie filling on the stove, using a small spoon to taste before adding more pepper and garlic. The mixture was coming together decently, and the crust was ready and crimped. Mostly, he hoped Brandon and what's-her-name would like it. *Note to self: find out Brandon's girlfriend's name before she gets here.* He'd invited them to the holiday party, naturally, but they were heading home for the holidays. They'd miss it. In an effort to see them off, he invited them to dinner. That, he was excited for. As he stirred the filling more, he pulled out his phone.

What's Brandon's girlfriend's name? I forgot again.
Jade didn't text him back.
He pulled the pot off the stove to cool a little and wandered to the window, peeking out the curtains. The snow was gentle now, stray flurries instead of full-on snowfall. He wished he lived on the other side of the building so he could see the army of snowmen they'd created, solid after days of below-zero temperatures. Instead, he lived in the back. On the other side was Alex. Somehow, he didn't think Alex appreciated them quite as much, but then he kicked himself for thinking so negatively. For all he knew, Alex liked snowmen. Or was at least indifferent to them. He didn't really know. Maybe Alex was hard to understand.

In the snow, there was one lone snowman, lined up, almost perfectly facing his window. For a moment, he thought the placement could have been done intentionally. He tried to wipe the thought from his mind. *Okay, Carly Simon. Let's not be so vain, shall we?* A sign, draped on the waving snowman, fluttered in the breeze.

THANK YOU

There wasn't a signature, nor was there any way Nicholas could know for sure, but only one person he knew would have gone to that trouble. *Doesn't take a rocket scientist to figure out who.* He smiled and nodded to himself. Without letting himself second-guess his next move, he crossed the hall to Alex's apartment.

Maybe he wasn't looking forward to being the third wheel at dinner in his own apartment, and maybe asking Alex to come over was the right thing to do, especially since he could let Alex know he'd gotten the message. It didn't matter. Any excuse was a good enough excuse to convince him to make a move. He'd been looking for reasons and these were solid ones. Nicholas knocked, then knocked a second time. Once again, he got no response. Maybe he was wrong about the snowman after all.

Alex couldn't believe he was going through this much trouble for a party he wasn't sure he wanted to attend. The store had been completely sold out of ugly sweaters, so he had no choice but to go the do-it-yourself route, but the attempt wasn't going as planned. He plugged the hot glue gun in and inspected it. Did it get warm right away? Was there some kind of switch? Alex was skilled at many things, and he was a scientist. A simple craft shouldn't have been hard, but for some reason, the ability to work the glue gun eluded him. He turned the packaging over in his hands, finding no instructions, so he played around with the glue sticks. The tip started leaking onto the sweater before he could pull the trigger. He decided he would attach tinsel there first, since he'd already gotten glue all over the shirt. There wasn't exactly another choice. "This is so stupid," he mumbled.

He stretched tinsel across the shirt from one end to the other, gluing along the strand and attaching bows at random. The sweater was certainly ugly, and he was pretty sure he'd burn it after the party. He'd spent an hour at the store to find what he needed for it, and he'd been so focused on buying the sweater supplies and a wreath that he'd forgotten to buy the gloves and coat he went to the store for. He didn't know why he was so invested in the party or the decor, but for a moment he wished he'd taken the lack of available ugly sweaters as a sign. "This is stupid," he repeated to himself.

At least he'd remembered to pick up a treat. There were no cookies left that late in the evening, but he hoped the white chocolate raspberry cake balls he'd found in the back of the bakery case would suffice.

"Ow, ow, ow, ow!" he yelped, pulling his hand back. A string of molten hot glue connected him to the glue gun. "Jeez." He peeled the drying glue off of his skin and examined the red mark left behind. Yup, he should have stayed home. This was far from worth it.

As he started to glue on Christmas ornaments—actual ornaments, made for a tiny tree—he heard a loud clatter outside his door. At first, he ignored it. But the noise persisted and got closer, and he was able to make out singing and some sort of stomping. Down the hall, Nicholas and the girl he'd been with earlier, along with three other people, were stumbling through the halls scream singing Christmas carols. Had they been sober, they might have been in tune, but Alex could tell they'd all had one or two too many for their caroling to be very coherent. In front of his neighbor's door, they finished "Jingle Bells," then half of them started in on "Deck the Halls" while the other part of the group began "Frosty the Snowman." As they struggled to catch up to one another's song, they failed to complete either one and ended in laughter. Alex stepped into the hall, closing his apartment door behind him, taking in the cheery, drunken carolers attempting to spread holiday cheer.

As soon as the girl from the snowball fight spotted him, she took Nicholas's hand and practically dragged him toward Alex, the other three following behind and glancing at one another, clearly confused.

"What are we singing?" A shorter man beside Nicholas stage-whispered.

"Shut up, Brandon. We're not singing yet." She elbowed him in the ribs.

"Then what are we—" Brandon started to ask, but the girl on his other side started singing "Silent Night." Everyone else joined in without question. A cacophonous crowd, their sound was a far cry from the silence they usually sang of, the song typically evoking a soft, peaceful mood. Their caroling was endearing in spite of the noise, and Alex smiled and applauded in spite of their questionable quality. A few others in the hallway clapped as well.

Nicholas winked at him, reaching an arm out, between the people in front of him, offering Alex a small candy cane. He nodded at the door. "Nice wreath."

"Thanks," Alex said. He took the candy cane, and before he could say anything else, the entire crew was headed toward the next open doorway. Maybe Nicholas only offered the candy cane because he was drunk, but Alex thought it had less to do with alcohol and more to do with Nicholas appreciating his horrible, lopsided, lone backyard snowman.

Chapter Seven

Bad Taste in Men

Nicholas's living room was crowded, save for the one person he hoped to see. He'd been waiting, and he wasn't being the best host when he was so focused on a single attendee who wasn't even there. He ladled more of the cranberry orange punch Jade had mixed—a bit too strongly, in his opinion—into a red plastic cup. "He isn't coming." The party had been going strong for the better part of an hour, and while most of the hall was either at the event or back home for Christmas, there had been no sign of Alex.

"He'll show up," Jade reassured him.

"Everyone's here. He isn't going to." Nicholas took a sip, wincing at the strength of the alcohol. It overpowered the other flavors. As he turned from the table, he was ready to make the rounds. His mother didn't raise him to stand by the drink and snack table and ignore half the crowd he'd gathered. One missing guest didn't break a party, he reminded himself as he convinced himself to talk to the friends who had bothered to come. If nothing else, he hoped being a good host would take his mind off Alex. Their recent warm interactions didn't erase his memories of how Alex had been. How he might still be. Either way, Nicholas needed to focus on being a good host. He'd failed thus far, letting Jade do most of the mingling on his behalf.

But Alex stepped through the already open door and Nicholas abandoned his plan to mingle, stopping in his tracks. Alex made a beeline toward him, extending the plate in his hand. It shook, nerves apparently getting the best of Alex. He tried to steady the plate by holding it with both of his hands until Nicholas realized, jolting to attention to save him. "Here. I can take it." He put the treats on the table behind him, picking one sweet off the plate and popping it into his mouth.

"They're store-bought," Alex said, embarrassment visible on his flushed cheeks. "Sorry they're not cookies. The store was out of them. And sorry I didn't make them. I'm not much of a baker. Not like you are," he said.

Alex was rambling. Within his first few words to Nicholas, he'd already blown his plan to make his treats appear homemade. He'd gone to the lengths of removing the packaging and putting them on a plate. Alex resisted the urge to smack himself in the forehead. He shrank into himself, crossing his arms over his sweater, which made a loud crinkle as the tinsel and ornaments brushed against each other.

"Oh, no big deal. Half of these are store-bought," Nicholas said, gesturing at the table. "Have to say, nobody else got creative and brought cake balls. These are great. What flavor are they?" He picked up another one and bit it in half, looking at the filling.

The warm smile Nicholas gave helped, and he uncrossed his arms again, making as much noise as when he'd crossed them. *Way to play it smooth, Alex.*

"White chocolate raspberry, I think." Alex wasn't certain he knew how to work an oven properly, so he was relieved to know he wasn't alone in bringing something instead of baking. If a food couldn't be microwaved or was more complicated than a bowl of cereal or a TV dinner, he didn't usually eat it. Not living alone, anyway. His mom hadn't been much of a cook either, come to think of it. He'd grown up on boxed macaroni and spaghetti dinners in a steady rotation.

"I like your sweater," Nicholas said, moving on to a different cookie now. "You went all-in on the ugly theme! Oh crap, unless it's not supposed to be ugly. In that case, uh...nice sweater?" He chuckled, raising an eyebrow. Alex could sense the teasing tone, letting himself calm down.

"You mean you haven't seen me wearing this nonstop since I moved in? Ouch. Nice style assessment there, Tim Gunn. I'm so offended," Alex said. Nicholas laughed harder. "No, uh. I actually made it myself. I figured a little DIY was the only way I could make the thing sufficiently awful." Alex left out the part about the store being out of ugly sweaters, forcing his hand, and he left out the part where he'd intended to buy a coat and return Nicholas's.

"Whoa, you made it? You really did go for it, then. Dang. Next stop, the Met Gala red carpet."

"I tried." Alex shrugged, trying to brush off the compliment. He felt a little weird about letting on he'd made such an effort for the party, but it balanced out the lack of effort he'd made on the treats, so he let it go.

"You succeeded. Want some punch?" Nicholas scooped some into a green cup and passed it to Alex before he got an answer. "Oh, careful." He put his hand across the top of the cup, blocking Alex from taking a sip without adequate warning. "Jade makes drinks strong. *Really* strong."

"Noted," Alex said. When he tasted it, he pulled back. "Whoa."

"Yeah. I told you."

"You were not lying about this one. I'm going to have to switch to the cider after this one." He laughed. "Is her life goal getting us trashed, or…?" Both of them giggled as Nicholas picked his way through the snacks on the table. Alex followed suit, munching on a carrot stick. This was the longest they'd ever spoken, including their conversation after the gym. The snacks were helpful, occupying him so he wouldn't feel compelled to run away.

His fight or flight response was set firmly to flight. He came by it naturally—that's how his family ended up in LA in the first place. His mother's first marriage, the one to his dad, exploded pretty drastically. Her response to divorce was running, and within a week of the papers being signed, they had packed everything and were flying across the country to Los Angeles, their items coming by way of truck afterward. He'd spent summers at his grandparents' house so he could see his father, but running was in his blood. Hard times meant leaving and going far away. The anxiety he had trying to talk to Nicholas, which reminded him so firmly of his friendship with Mike? The feeling was more than enough to stir a nervous response in him.

"Jade is less Christmas cheer, more cheer by association and alcohol," Nicholas explained. He seemed oblivious to the mental war Alex was waging, the urge to run away playing in his mind. "I'm thankful she tolerates my holiday obsessions as long as I make sure there are a few drinks to help. Speaking of, sorry for the weird drunken caroling. It sounded like a good idea at the time."

"I enjoyed it," Alex said. "You were all very...very festive." His careful phrasing was intentional, the perfect way to make it an honest statement. He couldn't exactly say they were on tune, nor were they necessarily good, but festive? They were absolutely festive. "So, is Jade your girlfriend?"

"Oh, God, no," Nicholas answered. "She's like...my little sister. No, uh. No. She's not my girlfriend." He scanned the room for her and gestured. "Her girlfriend is there next to her, Veronica."

Alex nodded. "Cool." At least he wasn't the only one in the room. He could check Nicholas being homophobic off of his list of concerns at least.

"Jade is amazing, don't get me wrong. She is a great friend. But we're not, uh. We're not really each other's type. She has horrible taste in men, for one. Or, she has every time she's tried to set me up with one."

"Oh." His response answered a question Alex hadn't realized he was asking. "So...she's not a great wingwoman?" Alex was trying to stall, trying not to get flustered, trying to salvage the conversation.

"Hardly. Or, unless I pick the guy myself. Then she's pretty great."

"That's...that's good," Alex said. He shuffled his feet. "I need to... I need to use the restroom."

"Oh! Right, okay. Up the hall and to the left."

Alex figured catching his breath was better than leaving the party altogether. Baby steps.

"That settles that," Nicholas said, swooping in between Veronica and Jade with a cup of punch.

"What settles what? You two having a great conversation and making eyes at each other? That clear up your concerns?" Jade asked.

"No, I mean. He's clearly not interested," Nicholas said. "I came out to him, sort of casually, and, like, two seconds later he bolted to the bathroom."

"Called it," Veronica said. "My straight-dar is very on point."

"Shut up," Jade said, no harshness in her tone at all. "She doesn't know what she's talking about. He probably had too much punch and needed to go. Or maybe you threw him off, and he'll be ready to talk in a minute. Give him some space and what happens, happens."

"Okay," Nicholas sighed. This was a recipe for disaster. "Wait, what if he got the wrong idea and thought I said it to hit on him?"

"Were you hitting on him?" Veronica raised an eyebrow.

"That's not the point!" Nicholas said. But then he confessed, "Only if he wanted me to be." Veronica gave him a look. "What? He's cute! But if he's straight, hell, I'll take a good friend out of the deal any day."

Alex didn't need to use the restroom. He just needed to breathe for a second. What Nicholas said answered questions Alex had never intended to ask, and the baby carrot he had been eating felt lodged in his throat. The few sips of alcohol threatened to come up. He wondered if Nicholas knew his secret, if he'd been too obvious in some way or another, but he was hardly willing to be open with himself, let alone Nicholas. There was no way he'd know.

Maybe Nicholas knew from their moment in the snow—if it could be *called* a moment—or the conversation after the gym that there was a part of Alex asking, not asking, about whether there was some sort of spark between them, a spark that could start with, but eventually transcend, friendship. *Does he know how much I've hidden from the world?* Alex patted cool water onto his face, then looked around for a place to dry it off. He didn't want to use the hand towel. *He's simply making conversation, Alex. He's being a good host.*

Alex cringed about having asked who Jade was to him in the first place. It gave the implication he wanted to know personally. *You asked if he was taken. Sort of a dead giveaway, Alex.* He kicked himself, fearing Nicholas would think he was hitting on him. *You are hitting on him.* Maybe, if he'd let himself think that, but at the same time he absolutely wasn't. Alex wasn't sure he wanted to give off the vibe to a stranger, particularly *this* stranger. "Get it together," he said in the mirror. "Don't be ridiculous." Maybe Nicholas didn't think anything of his question.

As he stood in the bathroom, he splashed water on his face, then stared at himself in the mirror. He wanted to go out there and make an effort, embrace whatever was happening in his life as a new beginning. Here, he could be anyone he wanted to be. Clearly this wasn't a judgmental group. His family wasn't around to think less of him, so only his own hang-ups remained.

But the part of himself saying to keep his secrets quiet was a big part, a part that panicked and wanted to hide, wanted to run to his apartment and stick his head under a pillow. He had so easily misinterpreted signs before. What if this was like what happened before?

"These student loans are going to bury me, man."
Mike was flipping through papers, groaning in
frustration.

"I know. Mine too." Alex commiserated,
overwhelmed by loans of his own.

"I heard if you got married they gave you some
kind of financial aid," Mike said.

"You looking to get hitched?" Alex turned around
in the chair he was perched in. "You have to go on
a date first. Not swipe on Tinder and then never
send a message."

"Look who's talking. I'm telling you, if my
scholarship ends before I'm done here, you and I
are going to have to get hitched," Mike joked. A
jolt of electricity ran through his body. Was Mike
being serious right now? Surely not.

"Yeah, man. I guess we'd have to decide who looks
better in white."

Alex was bad at signs. Bad at ones that meant things
and bad about assuming things meant things they didn't.
He wanted to corner Nicholas under some mistletoe and
find out once and for all if Nicholas was hinting at him just
as hard, if their moment outside of the gym or in the snow
meant friendship, attraction, both, or neither. He ruled
the last one out. Nicholas clearly wasn't into him—he was
only being nice—and if he was, Alex wasn't out, even if he
was letting himself, if only for this moment, admit it to
himself. But he couldn't run away, whether or not he
wanted to. Instead, he took a deep breath, opening the
door and returning to the party, leaning against a wall in
hopes he could observe without being noticed.

"Enjoying the party?" *Damn. So much for being ignored.*

"Yeah," he answered as Jade leaned against the wall beside him. "It's great." His voice was too flat, too strained to convince either of them.

"That bad, huh? I think you need more punch, if you drink. If not, there's cider."

"Yeah. I could go for more punch," he said. He followed her to the punch bowl and ladled some into a cup. The drink tasted too strong, but he tried, hoping he could let his guard down enough to get out of his head. He wasn't sure what to say to Jade; he was bad at small talk, if his conversation with Nicholas was any indication. "So, uh...what do you—"

He didn't get to finish his sentence. The song changed from whatever had been playing to the forever-catchy "Jingle Bell Rock." No one was immune to the song, and cheers went up at the first notes. "I love this one!" she exclaimed. "Come on!" She grabbed his hand and pulled him to the middle of the room so fast his drink sloshed, dancing in front of him and encouraging him to do the same. He tilted back the remainder of the drink and put the empty cup on a table near him, covered in other discarded cups and a small Christmas village complete with fake snowdrifts. He danced with her—or less with her than near her—and for half a second he stopped worrying if he was making a fool of himself. He may have been a strange guy in a room full of people who already knew each other, but he wasn't letting himself think about that. He was pushing the worry from his mind and focusing on the fact that they all looked ridiculous. That, and on the sound of the music.

Nicholas's hands found his shoulders, turning Alex to face him. "You're a good dancer," he said, barely loud enough for Alex to hear him over the music cranked up to maximum volume. If everyone was at the party, no one could complain about the noise. Jade danced beside them, getting enough into Alex's bubble that he had to move to make room for her. Nicholas moved, too, like he wanted to dance near Alex regardless of where he was. Their trio moved out of the center of the room, letting others dance there. Instead, they were on the fringes.

"Hey, look up," Jade said.

Alex did, with Nicholas's eyes flicking up after. Somehow, Jade had positioned them under mistletoe without him noticing until it was too late. Jade was a crafty matchmaker, but Alex remembered what Nicholas said earlier in the party. *Jade has bad taste in men.* His anxiety crept in. Was he another in a series of men she tried—and failed—to set him up with?

"Mistletoe," Alex said, mostly because someone had to say something. He swallowed nervously. His palms felt sweaty, but he didn't step back. He wasn't sure what to do. He wanted to run.

Alex lifted a cup to his lips and watched as Mike kissed his third girl under the mistletoe that night. He was tipsy, effects of alcohol apparent in his subtle sway and glassy eyes, and well on his way to making choices he'd probably want to forget the next day. As soon as the girl walked away, Alex went to him, tossing his cup into the trash as he did.

"Hey," Alex said. "Looks like you're having luck over here."

"Eh, somewhat. Still haven't kissed who I came here to kiss." Was he hinting? Alex couldn't be sure, but he wanted to go for it.

"Still waiting?" he asked, watching as Mike glanced around the room. He read everything he thought was a sign, leaned in, and pressed his lips quickly to Mike's. They were under the mistletoe, after all. Mike hadn't walked them out from under it.

Shoving him back with two firm hands, Mike blinked at him. "What the hell, man?"

"I'm... I'm sorry," Alex said. He waited for Mike to say the kiss was no big deal, to say he was only thrown off guard. Instead, he turned and walked away. He didn't respond to Alex's apology texts the next day. When he did reply, he sent a quick "Didn't mean to give you the wrong impression about me." Their friendship was effectively done after that point.

"We don't have to...I mean, if...do you want to?" Nicholas stammered. "We can." Nicholas wanted to, but after what he'd revealed to Alex earlier in the evening, the way Alex had exited the conversation so quickly, after how he'd already run from barely a second of holding hands, Nicholas didn't want to push the issue or make Alex think he was coming onto him, unless Alex wanted him to.

"Do you, uh, want to?" Alex blinked at him.

"It's tradition, right?" Nicholas answered. Alex lifted on his heels a little and kissed him, chaste and fast.

Resting his arm on Alex's, Nicholas held him a little closer, wanting to show him he was fine with Alex deepening the kiss if he wanted to. But Alex cut it off quickly, and Nicholas worried he'd been wrong to push this forward.

"I need another drink," Alex said quietly, turning his back to Jade and Nicholas and walking to the snack table, glancing back shyly. Nicholas stood in stunned silence. He couldn't process what was happening. For a moment, he believed Alex hadn't kissed him out of any actual desire, but, instead, did it because of Jade's pressure and the mistletoe and maybe too much punch.

"Told you," Jade said under her breath. "That kiss was destined to happen."

"Yeah? Because look. He's gone. He only did it because of the mistletoe, J." He decided what he believed was true, and Alex was only doing what was expected in the situation.

Jade's elbow in his ribs disrupted his thoughts, though. Alex was walking toward them, two cups in his hands, and as he got close enough, he passed one to Nicholas. "Can we talk for a second?" Alex asked, nodding to the corner of the room. Privately, apparently. Nicholas glared at Jade, then followed Alex. "So, here's the thing. I sort of hate mistletoe."

Nicholas's heart sank. "Oh. Sorry."

"I hate it because it makes it seem like you *have* to kiss. Like you don't kiss because you want to," Alex explained.

Nicholas didn't exactly love Alex's clarification either. He should have dropped it, let them kiss and never clarified. Now he'd been flat-out rejected. He tried to hide how wounded he was, but he was damn near angry with

Jade for forcing this, for making Alex think his hands were tied.

"The thing is," Alex said, "I actually did want to kiss you. I figured you should know, in case you thought the kiss was because of a stupid plant." He paused and took a sip of his drink. "But because of the mistletoe, what I'm worried about is that you weren't interested."

"Wait, what?" Nicholas stopped in his tracks. He'd been in his head so much he wasn't sure he'd heard Alex right.

"I'm worried you weren't interested," Alex said. "Anyway, I should probably go, so...uh..."

"So, uh, what?" Nicholas asked. He turned toward Alex fully, dipping his head to meet his eyes. This time, there was no mistletoe there as Nicholas let his hand graze Alex's cheek. Alex tilted his head up, and—without Jade or anyone else egging them on—Nicholas kissed him. This time, they didn't rush the kiss. This time, their kiss and connection were real, something they both softened into, a kiss they'd been dancing around since not long after they first met. For a second, the party faded a little, music growing quieter, not because it had been turned down, but because Nicholas could feel the blood rushing to his ears as his heart raced. Alex wanted to kiss Nicholas, and Nicholas wanted to kiss him back, and they did, focused on each other for that few minutes. Who cared that they were at the edge of the room where anyone could see? As long as Alex's lips were on his, Nicholas didn't worry about anything in the world. His tongue grazed Alex's lower lip. Certain now they'd gotten it right, he looked at Alex earnestly. "Please don't leave yet."

Alex's response was more breath than actual sound. "Okay."

Chapter Eight

Drunk Tank

Alex stood in Nicholas's kitchen after the party, hands submerged in soapy water as he washed the punch bowl. The other guests had cleared out long ago, the punch bowl long emptied, and he was happy to help with the dishes. Staying to help gave him more time to talk to Nicholas and his closest friends after the other guests had returned to their own apartments for the night. Nicholas had done a good job of convincing him to stay for the rest of the party. He'd only planned on making an appearance and going back home. However, once Nicholas had introduced him to everyone, he was finally more comfortable, realizing this place could be home eventually. With or without the kiss and everything else, he felt okay in Omaha for the first time.

After the new year, he'd be seeing the people around him in classes, or maybe working with them on campus. Getting to know them and recognizing they'd be familiar faces later reassured him. Nicholas was especially fun to be around, and everyone he surrounded himself with seemed fun too. That was why he was here so long after the party ended. He hadn't wanted to leave.

Near him, Jade picked at leftover snacks, lifting a sticky green mass to her mouth, a holly candy left behind by one of the guests. Alex watched as Veronica shook her head disapprovingly as Jade threatened to smear the residue on her cheeks. They were cute together, almost sickeningly so. He liked how in love they looked, and Nicholas was staring at them too. He wondered if Nicholas hoped to have a similar relationship someday. Alex did. Tonight was a step in the right direction for both of them. He wasn't about to get ahead of himself, first kisses hardly enough to say what the future would be like, but the tide was turning in his favor for the first time he could remember.

A switch was flipped in him, like choosing to be here made this feel safe. He couldn't help but laugh and relax around the people Nicholas had referred to—in a spontaneous toast—as chosen family. Alex always used to think the concept was cheesy and ridiculous. Family couldn't be changed, he'd always thought. You were given one of them. Family was family, friends were friends, and the lines were clear. But after seeing how Nicholas interacted so comfortably with Jade and Veronica and a few others at the party, Alex started to see the difference. Given enough time, living in the same hall as these people, befriending them, being open and honest about himself? Eventually, he might consider them family himself.

He wasn't there yet, not by any means, still on the fringes of a group interacting with their own language, their inside jokes and ease with each other, but he understood how it could happen. If he made an effort for once, he could be a part of that. He wanted to. He wanted to stop running away from who he was.

As Alex put the dishes aside to dry, he turned to the conversation they were having. Nicholas leaned in, letting their shoulders graze. Alex looked around. Apparently nobody else noticed how close they were standing to each other. But to Alex, it felt like someone had plugged the Christmas lights directly into his veins.

He'd hoped if he stayed long enough, he'd get Nicholas alone for a minute or two, long enough to ask him to coffee. The later it got, the less likely getting him alone seemed. Veronica and Jade were flirting and enjoying themselves. For a moment, Alex wondered if they'd notice if he asked Nicholas right there. Probably not, but for some reason, he wanted to have a moment alone to ask. He was new to this, nervous. The last thing he needed was for Nicholas's friends to hear how awkward he was and call him out on it, make him falter.

"Hey, come here," Nicholas said, tugging Alex's sleeve. Alex had been standing there, opening his mouth and closing it again. Nicholas couldn't be sure what was on his mind, and perhaps he wasn't thinking anything specific at all, but part of Nicholas hoped he was open to talking. Having spent so much time hoping for an opportunity to get him alone, Nicholas didn't want to keep waiting to see if Alex would ask to talk to him privately.

"Okay," Alex said, following him from the kitchen to the living room, settling on the couch. The floor plan was open, and they were essentially in the same room, but there was space. "What's up?" Alex's voice cracked a little and his leg bounced with clear nervous energy.

It was...cute. He felt like a stupid teenager with his first crush, nervous to speak to Alex. In a lot of ways, this *was* like that, a first crush. Since his breakup the year before, spending time with Alex was his first big attempt to let himself have feelings for anyone in a while.

"Nothing's up," Nicholas reassured him. "I wanted to talk to you, just the two of us."

Alex perked up.

"I'm glad we're neighbors, y'know?" Nicholas continued. Alex's hand grazed his leg and he was hyperaware of his every movement as he looked at him. Nicholas was tempted to lean in and kiss him again, but he held back, hoping they'd talk instead. "I didn't think I'd ever see you again. After I ran into you at the grocery store, I mean. I kept thinking about you though."

"You thought about me?"

"Yeah. I was hoping you had enjoyed the peppermint bark. Or, hoping your friend had."

"Maybe my *friend* is waiting for the right person to share it with. You know, someone who likes peppermint. Do you happen to know any peppermint bark fans?" he asked.

Nicholas chuckled. "Me? Know anything about peppermint? Of course not." He nudged Alex and grinned.

"Darn. If you did, I was going to see if they wanted to get coff—" Alex stopped midword, cut off by the sound of the bathroom door opening. All four of them were still in view—everyone they'd thought had been in the apartment.

"What on earth?" Jade asked, then said, "Oh, Lord."

Turning toward the disruption, Alex watched an incredibly intoxicated man stumble into the living room, staggering until he toppled onto Nicholas's lap with measured precision, in spite of how drunk he appeared. Wrapping his arms around Nicholas's neck, he acted as if his action was the most natural thing in the world. He pulled Nicholas in for a kiss, fingers running through his hair as he held him close. Nicholas struggled to pull back, but when he did, all the guy did was pull him back in, eventually settling to rest his head on Nicholas's shoulder. "I missed you, Nicky. It's been so, so long." His words were slurred. "Why aren't we ever together anymore?"

Alex was struggling not to cry, or run, or anything else he would usually do in a situation like this. He didn't know who the guy was, hadn't noticed him at the party at all, but whoever he was, he had strong feelings for Nicholas. From what Alex could tell, Nicholas wasn't exactly rushing to push him out of his lap, either. Maybe running wasn't the right idea, but clearly he needed to leave.

Nicholas looked at Alex apologetically. This wasn't how this was supposed to go at all. He'd had hopes and dreams for the party, sure, and the whole event had exceeded his wildest dreams. But none of his hopes or expectations included his ex-boyfriend falling drunkenly into his lap and kissing him right as he was getting up the nerve to ask somebody out. His goal had been to jokingly ask Alex to get peppermint mochas, then invite him to dinner instead. Before Sean had stumbled in, he thought Alex was going to beat him to it too. Now, Nicholas was responsible for getting Sean home.

"Let's get you home," Nicholas said. He shifted him off his lap and onto the couch beside him.

"I can," Jade offered. She glanced back and forth between Nicholas and Alex, giving him the chance to explain what was happening here, to clear things up and salvage the opportunity to ask him on a date, but Sean let out a weak groan of protest.

"Don't wanna go with you. I want to go home with my Nicky." His eyes were half closed, limbs limp. Sean was draped all over Nicholas, leaning on his shoulder and drooling. Nicholas hated the wounded, confused look on Alex's face.

"Sean, go with Jade." Nicholas stood and tried to pull Sean up, guiding him into Jade's arms and trying to help her situate him so he could lean on her as he went back to his apartment.

"I want to go with you," he whined.

"It's fine. Take him. I have to go," Alex said with a shrug. He was clearly disappointed.

"I'm so sorry," Nicholas said, but Alex was already on his way out the door.

Whoever Sean was, he obviously had more history with Nicholas and demanded his full attention in the moment. Alex couldn't argue with that, and he wasn't about to wait around until Nicholas had time to finish their conversation. He only had so much nerve, and sticking around when Sean needed Nicholas went too far. He couldn't help but wonder what was happening in Sean's apartment, if Nicholas would end up doing more than just taking him home. In his mind, he replayed the reel and tried to remember if Nicholas had kissed Sean back. He didn't know for sure, but the kisses he'd shared with Nicholas blurred together with the one with Sean less than two hours later. After an hour of stewing, he was certain Nicholas was as interested in Sean as Sean was in Nicholas. Perhaps he was merely a holiday stand-in for the person Nicholas really wanted to spend the evening with. Whatever it was, he'd let himself get caught up in it, the mistletoe and the holiday cheer he'd been so strongly against. He'd let Nicholas's spirit and excitement get the best of him. There was one thing he needed to remember to survive the holidays: don't give in. He shut his apartment door so hard a few ornaments from his wreath fell to the floor. Alex was certain he'd had his first and last kiss with Nicholas that night.

The last thing Nicholas wanted to do was play babysitter to the man-child who had broken his heart a year before, the one who had cheated on him and left him shattered. He was better off without Sean, and he knew as much now. At one time, he'd thought it might be the end of the world. When their breakup happened, he'd spent a full two weeks baking cookies and shoveling them in while watching sickeningly sweet love stories and lamenting on the phone to his mother how love was overrated.

Alex was the first person Nicholas had really had any interest in since. He'd long since closed those doors, and he didn't know why the little scrooge opened them, but he did. Finally, Alex was expressing interest, too, making this the worst-case scenario—to be pulled from their conversation before he could ask Alex on a proper date. Mostly, he worried Sean's clinginess gave Alex the wrong impression.

Not that he blamed Alex for leaving before he could stop him. The word *fear* was written all over Alex's face. Obviously, this was new territory for the poor guy. He'd just moved. Right before Christmastime, even. Nobody moved at Christmas unless they were running away from a problem or really intent on spending the holidays alone. If he'd come looking to start anew, Nicholas had to wonder why here, why Omaha? The Midwest was getting better at acceptance, but LA must be way more progressive. Weren't they? Alex must have been here for a new school, and nothing more.

Sean was the pressing issue. As much as Nicholas wanted to keep his focus elsewhere, he had a situation to deal with. Sean was drunk. Too drunk, really. Over-indulging wasn't unusual for Sean, but most of the time his current partner helped him reign things in, choose not to indulge quite so much. Nicholas didn't know where they were, but he could imagine things weren't going well at the moment. Sean could be like that sometimes.

Nicholas nudged Sean on the couch. "Get up, Lazybones. Let's get coffee."

"If it's not Irish, no thank you," Sean said, arm draped across his eyes. He was mumbling and annoyed, and Nicholas knew he was pushing when he shouldn't. He couldn't help it. Someone had to get Sean off the couch, and Nicholas knew it had to be him.

"Come on. I'll buy. You can even get a muffin if you want."

Sean removed his arm enough to let Nicholas see his eyes roll, then pried himself off the couch. "Fine, but next time I suggest we go to the bar, I don't want to hear a single damn complaint."

Nicholas knew begging Sean to go to the coffeeshop was playing with fire if going to the bar was attached. If he went, he was committing to being the designated driver for the bar trip. Someone had to, and it wouldn't be Sean. He didn't mind, but he also knew he'd be committing to babysitting his boyfriend and cutting him off after a couple of drinks so he wouldn't get all angry drunk on everyone. "You know what? Never mind. I'll bring you a cookie."

"Thank you," Sean said, flopping back on the couch. He knew how to get Nicholas to stop trying, if nothing else.

Nicholas hobbled through the hallways and into the elevator, half carrying Sean to his door on the top floor. "You got it from here?" he asked. Sean couldn't get his key in the lock. "Okay. Here. I'll help." Nicholas opened the door, putting the keys on the counter and guiding Sean in. He leaned Sean against the counter and looked in the cabinet for a glass. He used to know the layout of the apartment like the back of his hand. Thankfully, hardly anything had changed.

"Not gonna get me a beer?" Sean asked as he glared at the glass of water in his hand.

"You've had enough," Nicholas said, watching as Sean drank it to be sure he'd get *some* hydration at least. "Let's get you to bed."

"You gonna stay with me?" he slurred. He refused to do any actual walking, stumbling there and forcing Nicholas to guide him for fear he'd fall. Nicholas pulled back his covers, arranging him on the bed and shoving his limbs under the covers. "Fine, don't answer."

"No, Sean. I'm not staying."

The cry from Sean was unmistakable and painful to hear, a choked sob turning into a wail.

"What's wrong?" Nicholas asked. He hated these games.

"You don't love me anymore."

"Things between us were through a long time ago, Sean. We're not rehashing this right now. You're with somebody else now, remember?" Nicholas reminded him. "And I like somebody too." Nicholas fiddled with the lid to ibuprofen and set a couple of tablets on the bedside table.

"You and I look better together, if you're talking about the guy at the party," Sean mumbled, rolling over and kneading at his pillow.

"No, we don't. That's not the point. The point is you need to get some sleep, and I need to go." Sean whined again, and this time tears started to fall down his cheeks openly. Nicholas's heart broke a little bit. He knew the sting of rejection well, and as much as he wanted to relish in this moment of revenge, of payback, of cosmic justice, it was just...sad. Liking someone and getting rejected was painful, but the reality was by the next morning, when Sean was sober, he'd regret this anyway.

"You made me happy," Sean said, crying.

"Neither of us were happy. You know we weren't." Imagining things as better than they were was easy, if they looked at the highlight reel and ignored the low points and fights. The reality wasn't something Nicholas could easily forget. Even before the cheating, the bond they shared was a toxic one. Nicholas was happier after he got through his two weeks of hating the world and love stories and all things good. Once he got past the pain of goodbye, life was brighter and easier without Sean dragging him down.

"So you're going to go off and find someone new?" Sean prodded, as if he hadn't already done so himself. "He's what you want?"

"If you didn't ruin my chance, yeah," Nicholas answered, but Sean didn't hear. He was fast asleep, leaving Nicholas to let himself out.

Chapter Nine

One More Drink

Three drinks in—which was really two more than Alex should've let himself have—Alex was no more certain why he was moping as hard as he was. Three days had passed since the party, and he'd barely seen Nicholas, aside from passing each other in the hallways. Between his job hunt and getting ready for classes to start, he hadn't had time to seek him out, knock on his door and say *something*. He'd considered going to the gym, but they were crossing paths, and he was starting to wonder if Nicholas was intentionally avoiding him.

Alex had been stationed at the stool in the bar three blocks from his apartment for over an hour. He didn't see himself going home anytime soon, either. Obviously, he couldn't blame Nicholas for anything that happened at the party. Sean surely had a good reason to get trashed because of Nicholas, too, so he couldn't blame *him*. After all, Alex was at a bar getting trashed, which was all about Nicholas too. "It's not about Nicholas at all," Alex mumbled to himself, trying and failing to convince himself he was being honest.

"What?" the bartender asked.

"Nothing."

The sudden silence between him and Nicholas in the days after the party sucked. It only made things worse, that he'd been so close to the friendship he wanted and some drunk guy at a party had messed things up. *Or maybe that's on you for leaving.* Alex sighed aloud in the bar. *You're being ridiculous. Two kisses? That's nothing. Especially when one of them was prompted by a poisonous plant.* Logically, Alex knew he was being ridiculous. He and Nicholas didn't have a longstanding relationship, nothing warranting his current mood. But logic? He was pushing rationality out of his mind. Nicholas's attention was the most sign of interest Alex had ever gotten out of anybody, maybe because he'd been terrified to put himself out there. It was hard not to latch onto the kiss and want it to mean more.

They'd barely spent time together outside the Christmas party. The kiss should've meant nothing to him, some silly punch-induced kiss between acquaintances at a holiday party, something happening at offices and homes across the country all the time. Alex had to admit, though, for him at least, the kiss was important.

Nicholas aside, he'd never kissed someone so publicly, someone he genuinely liked. Or, he had, but this was the first time it had gone well. For the first time in his life, he'd been open about who he was, not hiding his sexuality from the world or the people around him. He'd let himself be fully, completely open, beyond the way he'd been able to brush off his first Christmastime kiss as a lapse in judgment fueled by mistletoe.

And this time he thought it was different.

Except like last year, it had resulted in disappointment.

Maybe none of this was about Nicholas. Or maybe some of it was. Or maybe all of this was about more than Nicholas alone, and instead about Alex and his war with himself and Christmas and everything spiraling through his head. He finished his drink and tried not to cry, waving to the bartender for another. He'd picked a drink with cranberry and orange because it sounded delicious, but the libation ended up being a little too much like the punch Jade made for the party. All it did was aid in his self-loathing and wallowing at the bar, thinking about his stupid mistakes and desires. The taste of the drink only served to send his mind spiraling back to the moment Sean stumbled from the bathroom. Alex had to muster the courage to kiss Nicholas in a room full of people. Before that, when he'd moved here from LA, back when he'd been so good at hiding his sexuality from the world, he'd felt weak. He tried to convince himself this was an improvement and a step up, Nicholas or no.

His emotional drain wasn't anyone's fault. This was just how Christmas was. His hatred for the holiday started to make sense to him. Christmas was the season of hopes and dreams followed by soul-crushing disappointment.

His mother's divorce and spiral into her depression.

His own selfish indulgence followed by heartache.

Now this.

He'd chosen this specific bar to get away from Christmas, rather than the one a block closer to his apartment. This bar was void of any sign of Christmas outside of the special drink in his hand. As he started in on his fourth, he wondered if he'd made the right choice to come to Omaha at all. He'd applied to other programs. This one had simply been his first ticket out of LA, but Omaha wasn't the only option he had. Maybe he could still transfer, change his mind and go somewhere else, anywhere else but here, as far from LA and Omaha as he could get. He'd only barely met Nicholas. He tried to convince himself he'd quickly forget the tall, impossibly cheerful, insanely handsome man. If only doing so were easy. "Ugh."

"Hey, Alex."

Alex jumped at the familiar voice beside him, startling a little. Jade was about as close to the last person he wanted to see as she could get. After all, seeing her made him think of...yeah, he might need another drink. "Hey," he answered. He stayed focused on a speck of dust on the counter, anything to avoid looking at her. He trained his eyes on the dust like he was attempting to set it on fire, like he actually could if he thought hard enough.

"You all right?" she asked, leaning against the counter and waiting for the bartender to come closer so she could order, arms crossed casually, leather jacket bunching up.

"I'm...yeah, I'm great. Thanks." Alex was lying through his teeth. It occurred to him then that almost every conversation he'd had with her had been filled with lies. He'd lied at the mailboxes before the party, and he was lying now. Of course he wasn't okay. He wasn't anywhere near okay. He also wasn't entirely sure why he was so unwilling to tell her he wasn't. "Actually, no. I'm not really okay." Perhaps the alcohol was having an effect, but mostly Alex was tired of always having his guard up. Jade seemed like a safe person to confide in.

"Want to talk about it?" Mercifully, she didn't ask if this was about the Christmas party. Maybe she'd forgotten what had happened by now, knowing he couldn't assume anyone else would be dwelling on the party like he did. She turned toward the bartender and said, "One beer and one Coke, please."

"I don't want to interrupt your evening," Alex said quietly.

"Veronica can wait for her Coke. Talk to me."

"You know when I kissed Nicholas under the mistletoe?" He paused. He wasn't willing to look at her, but out of the corner of his eye he could see her nod. "That was uh...the uh...it was the first time I'd ever kissed a guy that...y'know. Publicly. Or, the second time, but Nicholas is the first one who didn't push me away and call me weird." He willed himself not to cry. "Sorry. It probably sounds really dumb admitting that. I'm sorry." He had enough drinks in him to not filter his words, but not enough to be okay with the words he'd said once they'd left his mouth. He was ashamed even talking about it. He'd never actually said the word out loud, not about himself. Anyone might have thought, coming from LA, he'd have felt comfortable or normal with that word.

But living in LA didn't mean he hadn't been born and brought up in the South before his mother moved them, didn't mean he didn't spend his summers there growing up after that. To him, there was still a voice in his head that his sexuality, hidden as it may be, wasn't okay. His mother was cordial to anyone they knew, including gay friends she made at work or wherever else, but she also always whispered the word gay like it was a curse word, acted like anyone who wasn't straight should be ashamed of that fact. Alex internalized the shame and refused to let himself be open about who he was. He told Jade about Mike and the kiss the year before, and about how this was different. He choked on his words and blinked back tears. "I've never...never been open about being...gay before."

"That's a huge deal, Alex. You know I had a similar experience when I was out with friends my freshman year of undergrad. We were all tipsy, and one of the girls kissed me to get a guy all stirred up to notice her. I didn't realize her motives. When we got back to her place, I tried to kiss her again, and she freaked out, asking what the hell I thought I was doing. For her, the whole thing had been for show. For me, kissing her sort of meant something."

"That's awful," Alex said.

"The point is, we're at a distinct disadvantage sometimes. When straight people hit on someone, if the person isn't interested, it's no big deal. When we do it, people act like we're showing some kind of predatory behavior." She sighed and rested her hand on his arm gently. "Alex, it's brave of you to put yourself out there. Especially when you'd been shunned for it before. I'm going to take away any doubt you might have right now. Nicholas is into you. With everything that happened after, I'm afraid you might not realize it. Don't give up, okay? On being who you are, or on Nicholas."

"I was going to try to ask him out sometime," Alex confessed. He turned away again and tried to find the speck of dust he'd been so focused on before. "But, uh, Sean said he and Nicholas were...they were together? I don't know. I didn't want to get in the way of what they have, I guess."

"Have you talked to Nicholas about Sean and the whole situation there?"

"No." Alex shrugged. "I didn't."

"It's over, buddy. Has been for a long time. Sean knows that."

"Yeah, I could tell by how he acted at the party," Alex said. "If he knows, he sure as heck didn't seem like he was okay with it being over." He drained his glass and wondered if he could order another or if he was best cutting himself off where he was. He'd already blown his budget and then some.

"Sean left Nicholas. Did you know that? I'm sure if you talked to Nick he'd tell you the whole story, but Sean's one of those guys who can never be happy with what he's got. He's a good guy most of the time, but being a good guy and a good guy for the people he's with are two different things."

"Sean likes him. He made that pretty clear."

"It's not mutual, trust me." Jade smirked. "If you don't believe me, you can ask Nicholas yourself."

That was fair. The story wasn't hers to tell, and it made sense if she would rather he talk to Nicholas. "Thanks," he said.

"You're not going to, are you?"

"Is it obvious?"

"Yeah. You know, he was going to ask you out too. He told me after you left, some story about peppermint mochas and there being some sort of running joke between you two about that? I don't know. Don't tell him I told you. Let him think the whole thing was a surprise." She waved her hand dismissively. "What I do know is you're going to have to give him a chance if you want him to prove you wrong about what he thinks of Sean. Oh, and I also know you're giving me your keys. Veronica can drive us home later."

"I walked here," he said. He wasn't lying. He had Nicholas's coat draped on the back of the stool he was in and everything. He had walked to avoid making any worse decisions than drinking to forget his Nicholas and Omaha and everything that had come before it for a few hours.

"Well, you're riding with us. It's too cold to walk back. But first you're playing darts with us."

"I'm awful at darts."

"Prove it," she said.

Alex couldn't refuse the challenge, but prove it, he did. Within ten minutes, he'd accidentally thrown a dart at a board three down from where they were playing, narrowly missing another person who happened to be collecting his darts at the board. Alex wouldn't have been better at darts sober either. He had a long record of being bad at games like this. None of it mattered. Neither Jade nor Veronica seemed to care he wasn't any good. Despite his mopey attitude, they had fun, and by the end he was laughing with them. They were gracious enough not to mention Nicholas the rest of the night, all clear on how he was here to get his mind off of him for now.

At the end of the night, he was glad not to have to walk in the snow. "Thanks for the ride home."

"Literally anytime, babes. I'm the go-to DD. Hell, hand J your phone and have her put my number in there. You get in a pinch, you call me."

Alex smiled and passed his phone to the front of the car, letting Jade add both of their numbers.

"She's a volunteer at a shelter near here. She's seen more than a few people messed up after drunk-driving accidents, so she's pretty cautious. Aren't you, love?" Jade said, passing the phone back. As Alex went to put the phone in his pocket, he noticed she had scrolled halfway down the contract screen to show him the other number she'd added: Nicholas. He wasn't sure he'd ever have the nerve to text him and ask for a date, but he was happy to have the number in spite of everything. Or maybe, because of it.

Chapter Ten

Nothing for Christmas

Alex hadn't been in this particular grocery store since he'd met Nicholas for the first time. He hadn't stopped to think about that fact until he found himself parked in front of it, willing himself inside to shop for Christmas dinner. He'd decided he wasn't willing to swallow his pride enough to go home for the holidays, and he was too honest with himself to go to his grandparents' house either. Spending Christmas alone was less than ideal, but it beat the alternatives, and he'd originally planned to anyway. Alex forced himself through the cold air, into the store.

It took him no time at all to fill his basket with junk food. Anything remotely comforting, he had in hand. He was trying not to think about how he hadn't texted Nicholas, despite Jade's encouragement. He'd meant to, but the execution was a little fuzzy. He didn't know how to ask, or if he should knock on his door and say, "Hey, sorry I assumed you were still into the guy drunkenly kissing you. Wanna get coffee?"

Instead, he kept the distance they'd unintentionally crafted. If Nicholas was interested, Alex figured he'd have made a move beyond taping a candy cane to his door, beyond placing the fallen ornaments back onto his wreath. Maybe Nicholas would have said hello, done *something,* but he hadn't. Not really. But, as Alex pushed his cart, he realized Nicholas had made more of an effort than he had. Expecting more was unfair on his part. He resolved to go across and ask him to coffee after he got home from the store. Probably. Maybe.

Alex's heart leapt, then sank, at the display of peppermint bark he saw as he turned the corner. The shelves were restocked in advance of Christmas, a far cry from the near-empty ones that had been there when he'd met Nicholas in their minor tug-of-war over the last box. He put a box in his cart anyway. Sure, he wasn't a fan, and he had an untouched box from Nicholas at home, but he felt compelled to get it. With Christmas approaching, he'd be stuffing down the peppermint bark and all other forms of comfort food as he spent time alone.

He rationalized that eating the sweets would fill his emotional void, but that particular sweet evoked memories of Nicholas, the emotions there, ones he couldn't escape from. Debating, he stared at the box for too long, head cocked to one side as he bit his lip. *No. You don't need more sugar.* Another box of peppermint bark would tempt him to keep wallowing. *Time to move on, man.*

He turned his attention on the reason he'd come: Christmas dinner. He needed to focus. Obviously, he had no intention of fixing a full Christmas dinner for himself, but buying deli meat for turkey sandwiches wouldn't hurt. As long as his meal had turkey, some kind of vegetables, and a type of dessert, it counted, right? He had to hope so. As it stood, a store-bought dinner was his only option. The store was crowded, and he usually hated that. This time, the chatter and movement was arguably better than the silence of his apartment, where he'd been sitting alone in the dark all afternoon.

He turned down an aisle in hopes of finding any dinner option he could cook other than a sandwich. *Turkey Vegetable Soup.* The label stood out to him, and he decided on that, picking up a can, two, three for Christmas dinner and the rest of the week. Canned soup for Christmas? Not exactly the best dinner ever, but it beat the heck out of turkey sandwiches.

"Hey."

Alex jerked out of his thoughts quickly, looking up to see Nicholas standing there. Now, there was no chance to chicken out at the last second, unless he planned to sprint out of the store without saying a word.

"Hi," Alex finally answered.

"So..." Nicholas started. He didn't continue, just stood there.

"I'm sorry about the other night," Alex blurted. "I didn't know the story between you two, and I still kind of don't, and it was all, uh... The whole situation was a lot to process."

"So did you?"

"Did I what?"

"Process," Nicholas said, cocking his head to one side.

"Oh. I don't know. It's kind of a lot to explain." Alex glanced around. "I'm...gay...in case you didn't know. Or, I guess in case the kiss didn't make that obvious, or if you weren't aware I'm kind of really into you, and oh gosh, I'm rambling. Sorry. I'm...yeah, sorry." Alex took a couple of steps back, suddenly aware of how close they were standing and worried about what had come out of his mouth before he could stop it.

"Oh. Um," Nicholas smirked. "Thanks for telling me."

"You're welcome, I guess. I haven't really told many people that. Haven't really kissed many people either.

And now I'm saying too much again." Alex bit his lip. Holy cow, he felt awkward. He'd come out in a bar and now a grocery store, both times horribly awkward. Was it ever going to get easier? He wasn't entirely sure.

"Do you have plans for Christmas?"

"I do, yeah," Alex said. For a moment, he saw Nicholas's face fall, disappointed. "I've got a super-hot date with this, uh, this can of Turkey Vegetable Soup. Pun intended."

"Pun?"

"Hot. Super hot date. Soup...soup-er?" Alex said. Explaining it only made his attempt at a joke worse. He held the can up, showing Nicholas the label, but instead, Nicholas took it from his hand and put the soup back on the shelf.

"Nope. That's not going to fly. Not to be bossy, but I'm not sitting at Christmas dinner knowing you're across the hall eating canned soup. Come over. Dinner is around two, and everyone still in town is welcome to attend. Me, Veronica, Jade, and a few other people..."

"Sean?"

"No. Not Sean," Nicholas said. His tone of voice was clear: if Sean had been invited by any chance, he'd be uninvited pronto. Given what Jade said at the bar, Alex was willing to bet he hadn't had an invitation in the first place.

"You said dinner is at two?" Alex couldn't believe he was considering this. After what happened at the Christmas party, and given his complete inability to play it cool around Nicholas at all, the whole situation could be a horrible idea. But he really wanted to spend Christmas with people. "Do I need to bring anything?"

"Yourself. Bring yourself. That's plenty to make it a special Christmas." Nicholas smiled at him—beamed, actually—and Alex couldn't help but blush in return.

"Okay. I'll be there. See you around?"

"Sounds good."

Before Alex could second-guess himself, he stepped forward and leaned in, giving Nicholas a small hug, then kept shopping as if his heart wasn't threatening to beat right out of his rib cage and follow Nicholas home instead.

Now more than ever, Nicholas knew there was pressure for this to be the best possible Christmas. He'd planned on making one pie, but now he was certain he needed to make a second one. Even though he was done with the rest of his holiday baking, he remembered how much Alex had liked the caramels, so he also grabbed ingredients for a second batch. If nothing else, he could make them after Christmas. He didn't know why, but talking to Alex filled him with a nervous, excited energy that left him wanting to impress, going above and beyond his usually already extravagant efforts.

When he got home from the store, hours after they'd run into each other, after he'd done the rest of his Christmas shopping and other errands, he tripped on a small box at his door. Placing his bags on the floor beside him, he fiddled with the key, then picked up the box and saw the attached note.

I saw this and thought you might like it. Who knows? Maybe my heart is going to grow three sizes this season or something cheesy like that. See you on the 25th.

There wasn't a signature, but none was necessary. There was only one person who would attach a note like that to a box of peppermint bark at his door, the only person he *really* wanted to spend Christmas with. He walked inside and scribbled a note, then tucked it into Alex's wreath.

I happen to like cheese, Mr. Grinch.

Chapter Eleven

Unexpected

Alex was not going to Christmas dinner without bringing anything. Regardless of Nicholas's insistence, both at the store and when they'd passed each other in the hallway on Christmas Eve, he was determined to bring *something*. He stood in the liquor store, trying to decide which wine to bring. He didn't know what Nicholas's guests would like, and with Nicholas saying he shouldn't bring anything, he didn't feel like he could ask. Instead, he stared and browsed. Texting Jade was no help; she didn't answer. Eventually, he selected his favorite red and his favorite white. He hoped one or both would work, and if Nicholas already had wine for dinner? Maybe they could enjoy these together sometime. He convinced himself that wasn't why he was buying it.

Outside of family, Alex had never spent Christmas with anyone special. He'd never spent the holiday with people he felt particularly inclined to spend it with either. All the Christmas dinners at his ex-step-family's house growing up, for example, weren't for fun and giggles. But this time, he got to choose where he wanted to be, and a tingle of excitement coursed through him, a jolt of joy. After a season where he'd let himself be more or less untouchable, he let contentment consume him.

Though Nicholas said nothing about gifts, Alex couldn't resist the mini candy canes at the front of the store, buying a box of them for his host. With a bow and a little wrapping, he was sure Nicholas wouldn't actually protest. The gift wasn't much, just a small treat he knew Nicholas would love.

His execution was shaky, though, as if he'd forgotten his complete inability to wrap gifts. He tried more than once, cutting, taping, ripping it all off and starting again. He even watched online tutorials to no avail. By the time he got to the end of the roll of wrapping paper, he found himself driving—on Christmas Eve—back to the store for a gift bag. Most of them were sold out, but he got two of them in hopes one would work. Neither of them fit. His frustration was palpable, the growl of discontent erupting from him as he shoved the gift and tattered wrappings away. "Gah! It shouldn't be this frickin' hard!" The knock at the door didn't snap him out of his frustration, either, and he stalked over, yanking it open. "Yes?"

"Sorry," Jade said, raising her hands. "Didn't mean to interrupt a personal moment. You all right?"

"Yeah, sorry. You didn't interrupt. I've been trying to wrap this gift all day, and then I got the wrong bag, and it's not a major gift but I want it to look—"

"Okay, slow down." She shook her head and stepped in around him without waiting for an invitation, spotting the pile of wrapping wreckage right away. "You want help?"

"Please," he conceded.

Jade used the very last strip of barely-marred wrapping paper to cover the box easily, flawlessly, a seamless flat wrapping job. After she carefully peeled the backing on the bow, she secured it to the top right and presented the wrapped gift to him with a flourish. "Better?"

"How did you do that?" he asked, completely in awe. He'd been trying for hours to make the wrapping look okay. She had spent all of thirty seconds on it.

"A lot of practice. I had a big family, and I work in retail." She watched as he wrote Nicholas's name on a tag carefully. "You're coming to his dinner tomorrow?"

"Wouldn't miss it." He was happy to answer so certainly. He'd be there, and he was proud they'd managed to talk things out. He was also proud he'd decided to go without much prodding on Nicholas' part.

"Good. If you weren't, I was mostly coming to convince you that you had to. I've been worried about the two of you."

"Worried?"

"Neither of you seem particularly inclined to talk things through. I keep urging you both to talk to each other, and I'm getting crickets," she sighed.

"Crickets?"

"You know, dead air. Neither of you are saying anything." She shook her head. "It's clear you're a city boy. Sometimes in the country, it gets really quiet and all you hear are crickets. That's what trying to get you two to talk to each other is like. I didn't tell him why the kiss was such a big deal for you, by the way. Your sexuality and your story are yours to tell. And you *should* tell him. He deserves to know it was your first...y'know, with meaning." She smirked.

"Oh my gosh, he didn't tell you?" he asked. Jade's blank expression said plenty. "I came out to him in the middle of the grocery store. Just blurted 'I'm gay.' It couldn't have gotten more awkward," he lamented. "I mean, I couldn't have thought of a better way to come out? No, of course not. What's wrong with me?"

Jade cracked up. "Don't worry. I came out to Veronica the same way. I worked in a coffee shop, and she walked in, short hair, sunglasses, a denim jacket covered in pins, and I saw her and she started to order, and I said, 'Hi, I'm gay,' instead of 'Hi, I'm Jade.' I thought I might die of embarrassment until she came back the next day and gave me her number." She smiled, a genuine, accepting, loving look that made Alex feel seen and comforted in his awkwardness. "You know, Nick comes off as a really cheery guy, but deep down he's a pretty shy dude. Sometimes you have to pull the conversation out of him. I wouldn't panic about saying the wrong thing around him."

"He doesn't act shy," Alex said, but he second-guessed it. She knew him better. "Really? He's shy around *me?* Why?"

"I think you intimidate him a little. In a good way, I mean. I think you challenge him and make him realize getting to know you is worth the chase. Usually when he gets shot down, he panics and doesn't try again. There's something different about you, Alex. I'm not sure what, but there is."

"I can't imagine him ever being intimidated by anyone," Alex said. He shook his head, thinking about how tall Nicholas is, how imposing he could be in spite of his friendly nature, how he seemed to be everywhere at all times, bright eyes glimmering. Shy wasn't a word Alex would have ever picked to describe the man willing to sing Christmas carols in the middle of a grocery store or leave secret treats for half of the apartment building. But then he thought beyond the surface, the way he ducked his head to talk, the way he responded to getting called out with a quiet apology and a candy cane, and… "I guess I can see it a little bit."

"As long as you don't let his shyness scare you off. You're coming tomorrow, though," she said. "Don't you dare change your mind and skip at the last minute, or I'll march over here and drag you there by your ear."

Alex covered his ears, laughing. "No need. I'll come of my own accord. I swear! I already bought wine. I hope he doesn't mind. Nicholas said not to bring anything?"

"It's perfect. I'm sure he'll love it." She pulled him in for a hug. "Merry Christmas Eve."

"You too. Thanks for the help wrapping."

Jade was always so calm and careful in the words she chose. Obviously she genuinely cared about both of them, even though she hadn't known Alex very long. He appreciated that. He considered her one of his friends here, and he was happy she was willing to intervene so early on in their friendship. In that sense, Alex was lucky.

Alone in his apartment after she left, he set about fixing dinner. Was asking Nicholas to come to dinner too forward? He shook the thought away—it was canned soup, and Nicholas knew how to cook way better than he did. Serving soup from a can wasn't exactly the best way to make a good impression on the guy he liked, especially since he'd never invited Nicholas into his apartment before. He went back and forth and finally decided to ask. If nothing else, he'd be honest that he was inviting him for canned soup and see what Nicholas said.

He muttered to himself through the kitchen, "Hey, do you want to come for dinner?" and "I know it's store-bought, but…" While trying to figure out how to word what he wanted to say, he steadied himself and opened the door. "What the hell are you doing here?"

Of all of the people in the world he might have expected to see standing outside his apartment door, his ex-stepsister wasn't one of them. Still, there she was.

"I could ask you the same, Al. You ditch your whole family to come here right at Christmas? Really?" She'd barely been around for three years—off on a wild adventure with her boyfriend, but as she strolled into his apartment uninvited, with no explanation, backpack knocking his wreath onto the floor and sending ornaments flying, she was acting like she had every right to know what he was up to. "What's up with this?" She handed him a mini candy cane, tape still attached.

"Nothing," he said, stepping into the hall and picking up his wreath, putting ornaments back on all lopsided. "I'll be right back." He stepped inside and fished a bow out of a bag, walking across the hall and sticking it to the door alongside four others he'd put there the past two days, every time Nicholas left him a candy cane. "Okay," he said, stalking back into the apartment and slamming the door. "How the heck did you know where I was?"

Alex had told his mother, obviously, and his grandparents. But he'd never said a word to his ex-stepfather, or to his stepsister for good reason. He didn't want them to know. It wasn't their business.

"M—uh, Dad told me. I'm going to need to crash here for a couple of days. Bryan and I broke up."

"That's my problem how?"

"Your mom already said I can't stay there."

"For obvious reasons! What makes you think you can stay here *or* there? Go to your dad's!" He grabbed her suitcase and pulled it back to the door. "I'm sorry you're having a rough time, but you can't stay here." There was no policy preventing him from having guests, no rules saying she couldn't stay, but the thought of her being there crushed him. She'd shown up the night before Christmas. Since he couldn't leave her alone for the holiday, and he couldn't introduce her to his crush without outing himself, his Christmas plans were officially canceled.

Even if he'd asked Nicholas if he could bring a plus-one—and he knew Nicholas wouldn't mind—he didn't need his family finding out about his secret because she'd shown up and decided to blab. No, taking her wasn't an option. She was a loudmouth. If he took her to dinner, he may as well have mass-emailed the entire family. And all their friends. And half of UCLA. "Why aren't you at your dad's?" he asked again.

"He's crashing in his car again. Not a chance I'm sleeping in the back seat. But I found you, so here I am! Besides, look at you. There's not a single decoration in here. Are you planning on spending Christmas alone?"

"No. And I have a wreath!" he protested. She rolled her eyes. "Fine. You can stay tonight, but tomorrow, you have to find somewhere else to go." He wasn't going to kick her out in the snow, but he wasn't going to give up his plans either. Dana wasn't his responsibility. They weren't even close before she'd left.

"Tomorrow? You're really going to throw your sister out on Christmas?" Her tone sounded more like Alex had asked her to catapult herself to the moon—which Alex would have been just as fine with. "I'll find a place before the new year, but you've got to let me stay for now," she pushed. "Where's your guest room?"

"I don't have one. This is a one-bedroom apartment, which is exactly why you can't stay." Leave it to Dana to barge in and start making demands. That was so like her.

He wondered how she'd ever manage to backpack, being such a princess, until he'd seen her boyfriend's Instagram photos and the lifestyle his wallet afforded them. "I'll get you blankets for the couch."

"Fine. Are you making dinner?" She sniffed at the air. By the end of the evening, she'd eaten most of the soup and managed to wear him down with a casual "My back is so sore from the flight here," as she flopped down onto his bed, commenting on how he had the softest bed she'd ever felt.

Alex resigned himself to sleeping on the couch, a few blankets piled on. Of all of the Christmas Eves he'd had in his life—including the one where his mother had refused to leave his room, and the one where he'd lost his best friend—this was shaping up to be about as miserable.

Dana's constant commentary about his lack of decor didn't help. He started to worry he really *was* a Christmas curmudgeon. He hadn't been there long enough to decorate, but the realization was worrying. Maybe he and Nicholas were all wrong for each other. Nicholas was the epitome of Christmas cheer, and Alex had no idea where to begin with cheer in the first place. He couldn't sleep, and he couldn't stop thinking about how, in spite of his worry they'd never be a good fit, he wasn't going to get the chance to spend Christmas with Nicholas like he'd promised.

He got up and paced, unable to fall asleep. Eventually he pulled a paper from his desk and drew a candy cane, writing:

> *Sorry I don't have a real candy cane to tape to your door. Thanks for the ones you've been leaving. They're sweet. Like you, actually.*

I hate doing this, but my stepsister showed up randomly. I have to spend Christmas with her, which means I won't be able to come to dinner, after all. I'm sorry for canceling last minute. Maybe we could go get coffee some

"Can you turn the light out? I can't sleep with all your walking around," Dana called from the bedroom.

"Close the door, then," he snapped. He was sleeping on the couch, changing his Christmas plans, bending over backward because she'd shown up, and now she was acting like this?

"You know I can't sleep with it closed. Anyway, you need to get some sleep too, Al."

"Don't call me that," he said, but he turned the light out, hoping she would shut up. He tossed his unfinished note in the trash. Even if he wasn't spending Christmas alone this year, it seemed pretty obvious his holiday was going to suck.

Chapter Twelve

The Empty Place

Dinner was nearly ready and Nicholas couldn't stop shaking. He was nervous, but he was hopeful that not seeing or hearing Alex all day didn't mean anything bad. Not that he'd expected him to come until dinnertime, but now everyone else was here and his nerves were getting the best of him. The turkey was resting before carving, and the corn casserole was cooling so no one would burn their tongue. Everything was in place. The table was set.

Nicholas hoped he wasn't being too forward by seating Alex beside him. With how the table was laid out, placing him there made the most sense. But Alex wasn't there, and Nicholas was feeling the sting of rejection. Late was one thing. Alex was past late.

"He was late to the party too," Jade said, resting her hand on his arm. "Maybe it's a bad habit of his."

He took a slow, ragged, deep breath to calm himself. The worry must have been evident on his face for Jade to make a comment, but her assumption he was planning on attending when he was this late was outlandish to Nicholas. They were carrying the food to the table and he wasn't here. *He's obviously not coming.*

"Why don't you go knock and remind him?" Jade asked. "He promised he would come, but maybe the time slipped his mind."

Nicholas looked at the food and back at Jade, not sure what to do. The last thing he wanted was to be a bad host, abandoning his party for one guest. But in his mind, Alex was the one who really mattered, not that he'd tell Jade as much. Though, if he did, she'd probably laugh and tell him she already knew. "Everyone else is here, J. I can't leave." He didn't add that he would if he thought Alex might actually come, but he worried he was setting himself up for more rejection from Alex after things had finally started going well. "You go." *At least then I don't have to hear him reject me to my face.*

"Go. Seriously. I'll make sure everything gets to the table. "

"Please?"

"Sorry, Nick. He'll want you to be the one to ask. Trust me."

"Okay," he said. Her nudges were enough to ease the worry about hosting, at least. At the door, the candy cane he'd left was gone, and he hoped that was a good sign. He adjusted the "Merry Christmas" banner on Alex's wreath back into place after it had slipped somehow. Going against his better judgment, screaming this was a bad idea, he knocked. He couldn't keep himself calm, his palms sweating.

"Can I help you?" A woman Nicholas had never seen before poked her head out the door, standing there in short shorts and a tank top, like she'd slept over. His heart raced. Was Alex seeing someone already? Had something changed since they'd last spoken?

"Is Alex here?" Nicholas's voice cracked as he asked the question, the dryness from his mouth extending to his throat. He knew his ears were getting red.

"Yeah," she said, turning toward the apartment. "Hey, Al. Some tall guy's here."

"Hey," Alex said, stepping around her. "I'll be back." He closed the door behind himself, leaving her in the apartment.

"I wanted to see if you were um...still...still coming to dinner?" Nicholas looked at the ground.

"I tried to come tell you after I started to text you but dropped my phone in the sink. My stepsister showed up last night without warning. I didn't even know she knew where I lived. She's been glued to me all day, and I didn't get over there and...gosh, I'm really, really, really sorry. Please tell me I can make it up to you?" Alex genuinely sounded apologetic, and Nicholas was inclined to believe him.

"Of course. Do you two have other plans for Christmas?"

"Honestly? We're just hanging around here." He shrugged. "She um...she doesn't know I'm...y'know. Everything's complicated."

"I get it. Nobody at my place will say anything. Jade and I know better, so does Veronica, and nobody else knows. Come on, have dinner. Please?" He wanted Alex to know he had a way out, to say no, but he really didn't want Alex to turn him down.

"I can't leave her here alone. She's not from here and—"

"Alex, I meant both of you. There's so much food; trust me. I tend to overcook." He blushed.

"Yeah, I think I'm not surprised about that." Alex laughed a little. "Are you sure?"

"I'm sure. You shouldn't have to spend Christmas alone, so I'd love for you to join us."

"But we're already late. Aren't your guests waiting? I'm not exactly dressed for dinner," Alex said. He looked down at his pajama pants.

"So get dressed. We'll hold off on dinner a bit longer."

"Okay. Um...okay, yeah, then, we'll...we'll be there." Alex turned and rested his fingertips on his doorknob, then turned back to look at Nicholas again. "You're sure nobody else knows? Or will tell her?"

"I'm sure, but I'll remind everyone if you'd like."

"Thanks."

Twenty minutes later, and after answering a ton of questions about the guy on the other side of the hall, Alex managed to get himself ready and drag Dana along for dinner. He apologized profusely for the delay, but Nicholas promised several times he didn't mind. They weren't worried about waiting at all, he assured him. Alex could see the truth in the other guests' eyes, the way they salivated over the food. He could hear the microwave running, reheating dishes that had gotten cold.

None of that mattered, though. Everyone there was welcoming and kind. Nicholas seemed excited about the wine, and Alex was thankful to have a place to spend Christmas, even if having a tag-along wasn't how he hoped or planned his dinner would go.

His seat beside Nicholas was perfect. He worried his sister might correctly infer he had a crush on Nicholas, but Nicholas wasn't making a show of their connection. Based on that, it was as if they were neighbors enjoying a meal together and nothing more because that's exactly what they were. But being this close to Nicholas was downright intoxicating. He was tempted to slide his hand toward Nicholas under the table, to nudge him or take his hand, let him know he was interested in spite of how he leaned away at the table.

Alex knew he could trust Nicholas to keep his secret safe, and they sought contact where no one would notice. Every time they passed a plate or bowl, Alex grazed Nicholas' hand. Their touches were discreet, but obvious to both of them. Or, Alex hoped so anyway.

With conversation continuing after dessert and more than a few protests of "I'm full! No more! I can't eat another bite!" Nicholas was happy to have Alex's help washing dishes. He was thankful for him staying for more than the extra set of hands, because he'd hoped to absorb every second he could get with him. He longed to close the distance between them, wrap Alex into a hug, apologize a million ways about the things that had happened with Sean and with his own fears Alex would reject him.

He wanted to ask him so many questions, too, starting with whether or not Alex would want to go out sometime. Instead, he kept his hands to himself and resisted, leaning against the counter a few feet away. Dana talked to Jade and Veronica, but Alex stayed with Nicholas. Despite every reassurance no one would out him, Nicholas didn't miss the nervous glances Alex stole toward Jade, like he was afraid his secret might slip.

"Have you found a job yet?" Nicholas asked.

Alex's tension was visible, veins in his neck prominent as he swallowed heavily, glancing at Dana to be sure she wasn't overhearing even the most benign conversation. "No, not yet." He shrugged, as if trying to look casual. "I'm still looking."

"I'll keep my ears open for something. Cool?"

"Yeah, of course. Thanks." Alex's smile was genuine, especially with Nicholas following his lead and keeping his distance, not covering any sensitive topics. Nicholas knew he had all the time in the world to ask as soon as Dana left. *If* she was leaving.

"How long is your sister with you for?"

"I told her she was supposed to leave today, but that didn't exactly fly. It *is* Christmas," he said, voice hushed. "I'm not sure, though. Probably a few more days."

Their conversation continued mostly easy, even as Nicholas stayed cautious about what to talk about and what to leave unsaid. Goodbyes came too soon. As much as Alex wanted to hug Nicholas goodbye and thank him, he uttered a small "Thank you." Without making any contact at all, he turned and went back to his apartment, eyes landing squarely on the present he'd bought, the mini candy canes he'd forgotten to take with him. "Crap."

"Yeah? Forget something?" she asked, lifting the box up.

"It's not important."

"How long have you two been dating?"

"What?" He shook his head, hands up in defense. "We aren't— I'm not!"

"Alex. Dearest brother. Come on. You two stared at each other all afternoon, and you touched him every chance you got. I am not stupid." She knew what Alex wasn't willing to admit, what he thought was a massive secret no one knew. "Is that why you picked this tiny-ass backward city to live in? You two meet online?" Omaha wasn't tiny, but compared to LA, she had a point.

"I'm...I..." he stammered and struggled to find the right words to say, looking at his feet. "We aren't dating. He's uh..." Alex sighed and buried his face in his hands, muttering against them. "I met him after I got here, didn't know him before. It's a long story." He sighed. "Who told you?"

"Told me what?"

"That I'm gay."

"You did. Just now. Nobody told me anything," she swore.

"Does Mom know? I mean, not about Nicholas, but about...you know."

Dana laughed. "Do you really think any of us didn't know?" She stepped around the table and rested her hand on his back. "You're not subtle, Alex. We were waiting for you to be ready to tell us. Did you really want us to ask?" She leaned her head on his shoulder.

Alex's stunned look was something else, one of clarity. For so many years, he'd kept this locked inside, buried and hidden. He'd hardly admitted it to himself outside of shame-filled moments he tried his hardest to wash right away. His slip-up with Mike the year before had only made things worse. He'd pushed himself so deep into the closet he couldn't acknowledge it. How his family knew, he didn't know, but they *did* know, and apparently none of them hated him.

"Hold on a sec," he said. "I...I didn't realize... I didn't realize I was gay."

"Oh my gosh. Oh gosh. You're just now sorting this out? Like...now? This year? Holy crap, Alex. How did you not know?" She seemed stunned. In all of his efforts to convince everyone around him he wasn't gay, he'd done a good job of convincing himself. Mostly. Clearly, his family knew him better than he knew himself, or at least, better than he'd let himself be comfortable with.

"I did know, kind of, I guess," Alex sighed.

"I don't know if it helps or hurts to tell you we kind of figured even before Mike. But nobody mopes as much as you did about losing a friend, darlin'. I heard all of the stories about your moping from halfway across the world. Your overall crisis about the situation probably didn't help your secret identity at all." She was clearly joking with him. Nudging his shoulder playfully, she smiled. "Why not take these over there and then come back here and tell me what the deal is with you two?"

"There's no deal with us. Not yet. I mean, we kissed under the mistletoe, nothing else. I don't really know."

"Have you asked him out yet?"

"No," Alex said. He bit his lip, considering.

"Then get your ass on the other side of the hallway, give him whatever the heck this is, and ask him—no, *tell him*—you two are going out sometime. Your mother didn't send me all the way out here to check on you for me to let you chicken out now."

"Mom did *what?*"

"You know your mother. She was worried. That's not remotely relevant right now. *Go!*"

"Alex!" Nicholas seemed genuinely surprised to see him when he got across the hall.

"I forgot to give this to you earlier. It's nothing special." Alex kicked himself for the most awkward way to give someone a gift ever. *Nothing special. Way to go, man.* "I thought of you when I saw it," he added to make up for his awkwardness, shifting back and forth on his feet.

"Can you come in for a second?"

Nicholas didn't have to ask him twice. Alex stepped in, and now that no one was around but the two of them—a far cry from an hour before when the apartment was full of dinner guests—Nicholas stayed in his space. "I have a gift for you too." He handed him a small box, wrapped with the same signature care his own was.

"Jade wrapped this," Alex said, turning Nicholas's gift in his hands.

"You caught me. She wrapped yours, too, didn't she?"

"Yeah," Alex confessed, and they both chuckled.

Nicholas unwrapped his immediately, smiling. "This will get me through to the new year," he said. "I kept trying to flirt with you so hard with these."

"I know. I was hoping you'd understand I'm flirting back since I'm giving you a whole box at once," Alex said, blushing.

"Thank you. Seriously, these are my favorite." Nicholas looked at the gift he'd given Alex, and Alex got the hint, unwrapping it to reveal plain chocolate bark. "I wasn't sure if the peppermint was the part that bothered you, or chocolate bark in general, but I thought this might taste better to you than the other one."

"It looks amazing! I'm so excited to try it," he said. "Can I ask you a question?"

"There you go again, asking me if you can ask me things."

"Shush, or I'm not going to ask you," Alex said, biting his lip for a second. "Do you maybe want to go and get coffee sometime when you have time?"

"Maybe sometime when I have time? Or, uh...are you trying to ask me out?" Nicholas asked, stepping closer.

"Get coffee with me," Alex said, looking up at him, acutely aware of how close they were. "Soon."

"Okay," Nicholas said, pulling him into a hug. "This is going to sound so, so cheesy," he said into Alex's hair, "but I thought you'd never ask."

"Lucky for you, I happen to like cheese." Alex pulled back and lifted on his toes to kiss Nicholas's cheek. "Are you free the day after tomorrow?"

"I am."

If he wasn't free already, Alex sensed Nicholas was willing to change his plans to make time for them to go out. The way he pulled Alex closer and kissed him properly, not on the cheek but on the lips, cupping the back of his head and tilting his jaw up with his fingers in a way that left Alex very, very aware of everywhere Nicholas was making contact with him, spoke volumes. This time, there wasn't a drunk ex-boyfriend stumbling in to interrupt.

Chapter Thirteen

Snowed In

The snow was getting alarmingly high. Alex had never seen so much snow in his life. Then again, he thought "a lot of snow" was a few inches, but this was far beyond that. If he had to guess, he'd say inches was an understatement. Clearly, feet of snow had fallen instead. Getting to their date? Out of the question, given the weather. Alex watched from the window, seeing someone struggle to open the front door of the building, and the snow had already been shoveled once. The news billed the snow as the biggest winter storm in decades.

Alex had been counting down the hours until their coffee date since they'd planned it, but now there was no way they could go. Dana's flight had only barely managed to get out of the one-terminal airport the day before, ahead of the snow. Over a very long FaceTime session, she and her boyfriend made up. Alex wasn't sure their relationship would last for the long haul, but he genuinely hoped this was only a small hiccup in a long journey together. Either way, now that she was gone, she wasn't his problem anymore.

She'd been surprisingly helpful though. Outside of taking over his bed and his apartment without warning, spending time with her hadn't been as bad as he'd expected. She'd even sat with him while he called his mother and came out to her. Like she'd predicted, his mother already knew and was waiting for him to say something. All three of them cried, but they were happy tears, not ones of fear or hurt. He didn't believe the rest of his family would be as easily accepting, and his mother agreed not to tell them until he was ready, but the people closest to him had time to think about it before he came out, had time to grow and learn to accept him. In all honesty, they'd had more time to accept Alex than Alex had to accept himself. In a strange twist of fate—or maybe the season bringing people closer—Dana knew where he lived because his mother had told her father. They weren't back together, but they'd been talking. Her new antidepressants were helping her, and they were both rebuilding burned bridges. They were having Christmas dinner together. Maybe their reconciliation and renewed friendship would last, too, but even if it didn't, Alex was happy she didn't spend the holiday alone.

In an effort to keep up his relationship with her, he picked up the phone and called her on FaceTime. "Mom, you have to see this," he said before saying hello.

"See what? Your handsome face?"

"No, look," he said, showing her the snow. "There's got to be a few feet of snow down there."

"I'd tell you to get your butt back here to warmth and comfort if you didn't have a hot date planned. Maybe that will melt all the snow."

"I think the date's going to have to be canceled, Mom. There's no way we can go out in this," he groaned.

"Not if you get creative. You have a coffee maker! Invite him to your place."

The idea wasn't half bad. Alex considered she might be right. "Yeah, okay. I'll try. Thanks, Mom."

"When do I get to meet him?" she asked.

"Maybe wait until after our first date," he answered, laughing. Eventually, Nicholas probably *would* be meeting her. There was something about him, something good, and Alex hoped this wasn't going to be a winter fling. He realized quickly they actually had a lot in common, once they got past the surface differences. They hadn't had a date, but they'd slipped notes under each other's doors, starting with Nicholas leaving him a note saying he looked nice that morning—Alex hadn't realized Nicholas had seen him—and culminating in a note from Alex that very morning, saying he couldn't wait to see him. He'd left the note before he realized the snow was going to threaten their plans. "Mom, I gotta go. I'm going to ask him like you suggested."

"Bye, love." She waved and the call ended.

Yeah. Okay. You can do this. Walk over there and ask, "Nicholas, do you want to come to my place for coffee?" The snow was the only thing standing in the way of things going the way he'd planned, the only thing halting their progress, and even if he wasn't a happy camper, he wasn't letting it get him down. The minutes ticked closer to their date, and he hadn't seen a single snowplow drive by to give him a glimmer of hope.

"Okay," he told himself again. "Ask. It can't hurt." He opened his door, prepared to slink across the hallway and, best case scenario, ask Nicholas to have coffee in his apartment, or worst-case scenario, get a rain check. Before he could, he ran into Nicholas. Literally.

"Oh!" he yelped. He'd almost tackled the gentle giant, so focused on moving toward his door that he'd completely missed Nicholas standing at his own.

"It's snowing," Nicholas said.

"You're observant," Alex quipped back. "Too snowy to go get coffee." This was it. He was going to do it, going to ask Nicholas to have coffee with him. His hands shook a little, but he didn't think his face showed his nerves too much.

"Too snowy to go *out* for coffee," Nicholas said. "Never too snowy for coffee."

"Dang it," Alex said, scrunching his nose.

"What?"

"I was going to say the same thing but way, way less smoothly."

"Oh. Well, I was going to ask if you have pajamas. You need them. Trust me." Nicholas's eyebrows arched, like he was trying to picture it, to see if Alex was the kind of guy who wore pajamas. The look, the question itself, was intimate. Alex got goose bumps.

"Yeah, I do," he said.

"Okay, well go change. And then come over. I have coffee. And tea and cocoa. And don't worry, I have more than just peppermint tea. I got a few other kinds and—"

"Nicholas?"

"Yeah?"

"I can't change into pajamas if we're still talking about tea," Alex said. He grinned, and Nicholas gave him a small push back into his apartment.

"Go! I'll see you in ten minutes."

Alex took a slow, deep breath. "What the heck am I gonna wear if I don't have clean pajamas?" he asked himself, shoving away from the door he was leaning against and heading for his closet, yanking boxes out and overturning them onto the floor in heaps, hoping he'd find a clean set of pajamas. It took three boxes, but he finally found a pair of plaid flannel pants that looked decent. *Good enough.* He didn't have time to pick up the clothes strewn across the floor, but he could deal with them when he got home. He tugged on a soft, oversized white T-shirt and gave himself a once-over in the mirror. "Probably as good as you're going to get," he said, raising an eyebrow at himself and hoping Nicholas would like how he looked well enough.

Across the hall, Nicholas opened the apartment door seconds after Alex knocked, as if he'd been waiting by the door the whole time. "Coffee or cocoa? I have both." Nicholas greeted him without a real hello. Behind Nicholas, the apartment was dark, save for the twinkling glow of string after string of lights. They weren't limited to the tree, either, still up even though Christmas had passed. Instead, the lights stretched across the entire room.

The floor was piled with soft blankets and pillows, couch cushions, any spare piece of bedding Nicholas owned. Sheets were tacked into the walls, stretched across the room and clipped together in a few places to make a fort. Everything in the room was bathed in a warm glow.

Alex was in slight disbelief and shock. He'd planned to invite Nicholas over, but this was a million times above and beyond what he had considered.

"Alex?"

It took him several moments to realize he hadn't actually answered Nicholas's question, too distracted by the setup. "Oh. Sorry. Cocoa sounds great. Thank you." He couldn't peel his focus away from the fort.

"I was bummed when it looked like the snow was going to cancel our plans," Nicholas said, stepping behind

Alex and putting his hand on his lower back. "I thought changing our date a little might make it better anyway. I hope that's okay?" Suddenly, Nicholas's usual wall of confidence had cracks, like he couldn't be certain Alex liked it, like maybe he'd gone too far?

"It's beautiful," Alex said, stepping forward and reaching his fingers out toward some of the lights. The dim glow of the string lights gave the space a comfortable softness, like he should be whispering. The fort deserved reverence and gentle care. This no longer looked like the living room they'd first kissed in, lacking the hustle and bustle of a holiday party. It wasn't close to the apartment Alex had first seen, either, when he was grumpy over the loud music. It even felt a world apart from how he'd seen the room most recently, when they'd discussed plans to get coffee.

Now? The room was magical.

"This was the best I could do, since no one expected *this* much snow," Nicholas shrugged. "It was short notice." That much was true. The news reports had said maybe they'd get a few inches, but somehow the storm shifted tracks and buried them.

"I think this is better than going somewhere for coffee," Alex reassured him. Here, things were private, soft and quiet. They could talk and truly get to know one another.

Nicholas passed him a cup of cocoa. "Marshmallows or whipped cream?" he asked. "Or both, I guess."

"Both sounds good," Alex said, smiling. Nicholas dropped several mini marshmallows on one side and sprayed whipped topping on the other as Alex held the oversized mug steady in both hands. The decadence of having both wasn't lost on him. He liked how the flavors of the melted marshmallow fit in with the creaminess of the whipped cream. As he pulled back, whipped topping stuck to his top lip.

"You have a little—" Nicholas said, leaning in and kissing it off.

"Thanks," Alex said as he pulled back. The heat in his cheeks had less to do with the heater or the cocoa or the lights and more to do with how he felt about being close to Nicholas.

The blanket fort was perfect for talking, far preferable to a coffee shop where they'd have been separated by a table. Here, they relaxed on pillows, talking to each other face-to-face, and if they needed to, they were close enough to kiss the whipped cream off each other's lips. Small talk wasn't small when Alex shared it with Nicholas, never boring or basic or simple.

"What's with the mini candy canes, anyway?" Alex asked, sucking on the one Nicholas had most recently offered him. "Are they a seasonal thing or an all-the-time thing?"

"Seasonal, mostly. In the spring, I usually switch to lollipops. Honestly? I tend to be pretty self-conscious and having some sort of sweet to offer someone is a good icebreaker or a good deflection when I'm worried I upset someone. Except, you know...you turned them down a lot at first. It kind of threw me for a loop."

"Sorry," Alex said. "I wasn't trying to mess with your head. It's just, I'm from LA and a little skeptical of someone offering candy or gifts like that without a weird catch."

"I get it," Nicholas said. What Jade told Alex seemed to ring true: a lot of what Alex had mistaken for overly cheerful was a cover for insecurity and loneliness. In the same vein, Alex had masked his own insecurity and loneliness with a complete lack of cheer, shutting out the world and internalizing things as if he were above all this. Nicholas covered his fears by acting happy all the time. "You already called me out on the times I used them to flirt with you. For the record, you're the only one I was flirting with when offering them. Everyone else, I was only being nice."

"Good to know," Alex laughed. He patted the pillows and blankets around him. "So there's nobody else in the blanket fort with us? No other candy cane contenders I need to compete with for your heart?"

Nicholas cackled, pulling him in. "I mean, if you want to fight for it, I'm not complaining." He kissed him softly.

"Are you always as cheery as you seem?" Alex asked.

"I'm a glass-half-full guy, yeah. It doesn't mean I think things are perfect all the time. And it doesn't make *me* perfect. Like I said, riddled with insecurities."

"I tend toward glass half empty," Alex said. "If I'm in the mood to be particularly annoying, I like to point out the glass is always full, partly with liquid and partly with air."

"Are you particularly annoying today?"

"No. Right now, the glass feels full. Not in a snarky and annoying way, but in the 'I'm really, really happy we got snowed in together' way."

"I'm happy too," Nicholas said. For a long time, they did nothing but talk. They talked so long they'd have been kicked out for closing time if they had gone to a coffee shop like they'd planned. Alex couldn't stop talking, couldn't stop trying to get to know the curious, festive person from across the hall, and Nicholas couldn't stop unpacking the layers of Alex's mind and working to let his guard down.

"So you've never, uh... You've never been with a guy before?" Nicholas finally asked.

"Is that a deal breaker?" Alex's own insecurities bubbled to the surface again. He wondered if Nicholas would decide he wasn't worth his time, that dating a guy who was newly out and inexperienced would be too frustrating.

"No. I was just curious."

Alex had spent so much of his life at war with himself, in a silent battle between his desires and wants. Letting someone in was hard. But Nicholas was different, unavoidable, important. So, Alex told him about Mike, the whole story, how he'd tried and failed and pushed himself as far into the closet as he could. Nicholas listened intently.

"You know you don't have to get things right on the first try," Nicholas said. "My first kiss was with a guy ten years older than me. He was married, but I didn't know that when we kissed. I had only recently come out, and a girlfriend of mine took me to a club, and... It was awkward. Thank God all we did was kiss, you know?" He sighed and laid back on the pillows. "I think most people want to forget how bad their first experience is. But I think we had a pretty decent first kiss. And second kiss. Until Sean messed it up," he sighed. "I'm sorry."

"No, it's... You're right. Our kiss was good. And if that messed it up, then I guess this can be a good do-over," Alex said, leaning in to kiss him again. For a long while, small talk became deep talk became small talk again.

"What kind of music do you like?" Alex asked, an hour after they'd had a conversation about kisses and coming out. They strayed between topics, landing on this one for now.

"A lot of stuff. Growing up, I listened to whatever rap my brother was into. And I always listened to a lot of country." He leaned back and looked at the ceiling. "This is, uh. I'm so embarrassed—don't laugh—but I really love Billy Ray Cyrus."

"You're joking."

"I said don't laugh," Nicholas groaned, hiding his eyes in mock shame.

"I didn't laugh! I'm relieved I won't have to hide the fact that I own every one of his albums on vinyl."

"You do *not* have all of them on vinyl."

"I do. Want me to prove it?" Alex shifted, starting to sit up to go get his trunk of records, but Nicholas pulled him back down onto the heap of bedding.

"Show me tomorrow," he said. Alex liked the implication that he'd be too busy until then to show him sooner. "You want more cocoa?"

"Sure."

They stayed close in the blanket fort for hours, talking and drinking cocoa. After a while, Nicholas picked up his phone and scrolled through, turning on music instead. Alex whisper sang the words, fingers tracing Nicholas's arm. Lights twinkled above them in various lighting patterns, and though it was getting late, Alex wasn't set on leaving. Nicholas asking him to stay was a blessing, really.

It took Alex a few moments to figure out where he was in the morning. The twinkling lights above him were on, but now bright light spilled in through the window, illuminating the snow stuck to the corners. As he tried to lift himself up on his elbows and look around, soft cushions sank and kept him down. When he did sit up, he bumped into a small breakfast tray bearing coffee and a mini candy cane. An almost-empty mug sat beside his full one. He could smell bacon, too, and he stood up and walked toward the kitchen, coffee in hand. Nicholas was wearing pajama pants and an apron and standing by the stove.

"You cook bacon shirtless? I don't know if you're more brave or crazy."

"I have an apron," he said, turning toward Alex with a brilliant smile.

"Doesn't it hurt your arms?" Alex bit his lip and watched as bacon grease spattered, flying onto Nicholas's arms. Nicholas didn't flinch.

"I'm used to the pain. I love bacon."

Alex nodded. *The cookies. Of course he does.* He watched as Nicholas turned and dredged toast into liquid, then into cornflakes. "What's that?"

"Double-dipped French toast. It's my specialty, so much crispier than regular French toast. I never get to make it for anyone else, though. Jade and Veronica aren't morning people, so brunch is never an option." Alex started to suggest that he make it for dinner—there were no rules against breakfast foods at night—but his stomach growled in protest. He hadn't realized he was hungry until he smelled what Nicholas was cooking. Most of the time, Alex subsisted on cereal at all times of day, but he could get used to this.

"It smells so good," he said. "Do you have any sugar?"

"Yeah, of course. Come here." Alex did, and Nicholas gave him a quick kiss. "Oh," he said, winking. "You must have meant the granulated stuff."

"I did, but uh, you can give me that kind of sugar anytime too." Everything with Nicholas felt so much easier than he could have ever dreamed, so natural.

"It's in the large canister on the counter behind me." He tilted his head back to nod toward it. As Alex stirred it into his coffee, Nicholas worked quick, cooking the French toast as he loaded plates with bacon, sliced fruit, and the finished toast. He handed Alex a plate and grabbed his own, carrying the bottle of syrup and calling out, "Come watch a movie with me!"

"Okay," Alex said. He plodded along behind. "What movie?"

"We could watch *Love Actually*. Or, uh...*The Holiday*! They're my favorites."

"What are they about?" Alex asked. "I've never heard of either of them."

Nicholas affected a gasp and an offended expression. "You honestly mean to tell me that you—a guy I'm really into—has never heard of *Love Actually* or *The Holiday*? Oh, gosh. Oh, no. That won't stand. You have to watch both of them. *Love Actually* first. If I'm going to like you, you're going to have to have a basic understanding of quality romance movies."

"Both of them? Today?" Alex raised an eyebrow.

"Do you have better plans? Look outside and tell me you have anything better to do than cuddling and watching movies and eating bacon. We got more snow overnight, sir. Get your butt in my blanket fort."

Alex smiled and settled into the cushions. "Okay, okay. Both." He pulled his tray closer to him as Nicholas popped the DVD into the player and fiddled with the remote, setting the movie to play. "So, you're really into me, huh?" Alex teased. Obviously. They'd spent the night together, exchanged quick kisses, and Alex had laughed harder than he had in ages.

"Nah. Totally hate your guts. That's why I made you breakfast." Nicholas laid back and took a bite of his bacon, smirking. Alex kissed him, tugging at his lower lip until Nicholas yelped and pushed him back. "You're making us miss the beginning."

"Fine, fine, I'll watch." Alex lay back, eating his breakfast and giving his full attention to the movie. He tried to understand what Nicholas liked about it so much. The film wasn't bad, but holiday magic? He wasn't so sure.

"What'd you think?" Nicholas asked after, eager to know his thoughts. Alex shrugged. "Oh my God, you didn't like it!" He looked at Alex with mock horror. "There wasn't a single storyline you were on board with?"

"The storylines are the problem!" Alex exclaimed. "There were too many all at once!" He shrugged. "Like, okay. Say they make a movie about us. They could give us all the screen time, all the highs and lows of our story, or they could divide our time between ten other stories and tangle them altogether and add way more angst. Which would you prefer?"

"I don't know." Nicholas smirked. "Maybe I'm not a screen time hog, Mr. Ego." He laughed and leaned in. "You'll like *The Holiday* more, then, I bet."

There was no trying to get out of watching the second movie, not when Nicholas was already opening the case. Alex was going to watch, and he was determined to find a positive comment to make about the film. He wasn't sure how he'd ended up so attracted and attached to someone so into the holidays when he could be so indifferent to them, but in all honesty, he found Nicholas's charm and genuine excitement endearing. He had to admit Nicholas, when excited about Christmas, was adorable. Then again, he'd have trouble thinking of a time Nicholas wasn't cute.

With their breakfast long finished and trays discarded to the side, Alex was able to curl up against Nicholas during the movie. Nicholas casually draped an arm around his shoulders. The subtle intimacy was nice, comfortable. But every time Alex started to look at him, Nicholas guided his attention back to the movie. Alex didn't mind much. This one was better, he thought, but focusing was hard when being this close to Nicholas was overwhelming in ways he couldn't fully wrap his head around. As the credits rolled, he finally turned toward Nicholas, giving him his full attention.

"Was this one better?"

"Yeah. I liked it a lot more." He beamed. "But…it probably would have improved by Jack Black and Jude Law getting together in the end."

"Come on, you can't admit you liked it, with no catches?" Nicholas teased, giving Alex a small, gentle shove backward onto the cushion. "I even made a blanket fort like in the movie! I mean yeah, I don't have two daughters to share it with us, but if you want, I'll put a napkin on my face."

Alex laughed and traced his fingers over Nicholas's cheeks. "I said it was good—*is* good, really cute. I was saying it could have been gayer, that's all. What's the saying? Make the yuletide gay? There are a ton of Christmas movies, and you have yet to show me one that lives up to that."

"Oh, there are gay Christmas movies. Trust me. They're all mostly garbage." Nicholas stood up and pulled a box of DVDs from the bottom shelf and pushed them toward Alex. "Be my guest." He paused. "You're right though. Jude Law and Jack Black would make a really cute couple."

He lay down beside Alex, and Alex pushed the box away to rest his head on Nicholas's chest, listening to his heartbeat and letting his Nicholas run his fingers through his hair. He didn't say anything for a long while, then he took a deep breath. "You and I would make a cute couple." He couldn't stop himself from saying it, but the second he did, he turned bright red. If Nicholas had been listening to his heart instead of the other way around, Alex was certain he'd be able to hear it racing. Before he could open his mouth to change feet, to say anything to make the moment less awkward, Nicholas cleared his throat.

"You're right. We would."

Chapter Fourteen

First Time for Everything

Alex was more than a little nervous. He'd made it clear he wanted to do this, and he'd made the first move, but he still felt jittery. He did want to take the next step with Nicholas. He *really* wanted to. Moving fast wasn't the issue, because he'd been waiting for so long. Whatever this was, the pace was right.

The shaky quiver in Alex's breath made Nicholas hesitate, too, pausing for a moment as his lips brushed Alex's hip bone. He didn't want to push too far or too fast, push toward a place Alex might not be ready to go. But Alex *was* ready, and the way he tangled his fingers in Nicholas's hair, the way his hips bucked upward was all the encouragement he needed.

Nicholas let himself be guided by Alex's sounds and touches, his teeth and tongue grazing at the skin just above Alex's waistband. He'd been right—any of the gay Christmas movies he owned were less than stellar. They'd both gotten bored and easily distracted trying to watch them. Making out during a movie was nice, but now that their movies were over, they'd gotten more and more handsy until they'd gotten here, with Alex on his back, arching off the pillows beneath him.

Alex wasn't being demanding by any means, but the soft pleading whimpers anytime Nicholas's kisses reached his neck or his jaw said a lot about what he wanted. The way his hands explored Nicholas's back and chest, down his hips? It made things more obvious. Alex prayed his naivety wasn't apparent, that Nicholas didn't notice how new this was to him, even if logically he was aware Alex hadn't done something like this before. Mostly, he didn't want to stop Nicholas to say, "Remember, I have no idea what I'm doing." He let Nicholas take the lead and hoped to figure out his role when he got there.

Thankfully and unfortunately, Nicholas took things slowly. Almost painfully so, as if Alex might change his mind the second his hand went too far. But he wasn't going to. Instead, he was coming unglued and muttering a string of, "Oh gosh, please...yes..." before Nicholas had even undressed him. Alex's brain was short-circuiting as his body took the lead, moving without his mind giving him any clue on what he was doing. In the blanket fort, he was safe. Nicholas's strong hands on him felt beautiful and tender, guiding him softly and slowly. The moment was right in every possible way.

Alex realized he was pulling Nicholas's hair and guiding him down, and he panicked he was gripping too tight, hurting him. He struggled to free his hands from the thick curls, but Nicholas didn't mind, pressing his fingertips into Alex's hips and pulling him closer. "You can pull my hair if you want to."

Alex twisted his fingers into Nicholas's hair again, and Nicholas sighed contentedly against his skin. The flash of his eyes, the way he looked both hungry and at peace, set Alex on fire all over again.

"Is this okay?" Nicholas asked.

Alex arched his back and moved his hips toward Nicholas again, letting his head fall back onto the soft pillows of the fort. "Gosh, yes," he breathed, pushing and pleading as Nicholas slid his pajama pants down, exposing him to the warm apartment air. As he kissed back up Alex's body, his mouth lingered on the places where Alex had reacted strongest. He grazed his lips on his hip bone again, let his tongue flick across Alex's nipple, and pressed his teeth gently into his collarbone.

"Yeah?" was the only response Nicholas could reasonably give to the nearly incoherent babbling Alex muttered before Nicholas had touched him *there*. Sensory overload. That was the only way he could describe it. Nicholas's bare skin on his own overwhelmed him. Mixing the sensation with every soft touch and lingering kiss and the lights twinkling above him, and Alex was so far gone before he could ever make sense of things. He pulled Nicholas in for a kiss as Nicholas wrapped his hand around his length, stroking Alex gently, slowly, intentionally.

"Yeah, like that, perfect..." Alex groaned, speaking right against Nicholas's lips. The first touch alone was almost too much, and Alex tried to train his thoughts on anything to stave off his release for a few more minutes, to let himself become fully immersed in this moment. Nicholas kept a slow pace, picking up the movement when Alex's breath hitched, when his body trembled beneath him. Alex wanted this to last forever, but at the same time, he craved release. He wanted to try everything, but he also wanted to enjoy what they were doing right now. He wanted more, and he let his hand graze down Nicholas's bare chest and stomach, slipping it into his waistband.

"Not yet," Nicholas whispered. He stopped holding Alex's hand long enough to move, to hold Alex's wrists above his head and use his other hand to stroke him like he'd been doing. The pained and puzzled expression must have been striking to Nicholas. For half a second, he stopped again. "Trust me, honey. I want that. I want you. But right now, relax."

Alex wondered if Nicholas could sense how little he let himself do that—relax—and he could tell how focused Nicholas was on making this good for him, more than he was on getting any sort of reciprocation. "I— Oh—" Alex's words were cut off by a shaky, ragged breath pushing the air from his lungs. He had to wonder if Nicholas knew how close he was. He twitched in Nicholas's hand. For Alex, the sensation was nothing like the hundreds, maybe thousands of times he'd gotten himself off as a teen and young adult, feeling shameful later. This was different, dare he say magical, like everything about the past couple of days had been. Compared to his own hand, Nicholas was night-and-day better, different, taking care of him and tending to his desires. Alex couldn't quite put words to how amazing everything felt.

"You're beautiful," Nicholas whispered. His lips brushed Alex's ear and that was enough to drive him over the edge without any other warning. Nicholas rolled out of the position he'd been in, lying beside him. Alex tried to catch his breath, struggling, and he could count his ribs as he sucked in air, body shaking from the aftershocks of what they'd done.

"Wow," he finally breathed.

"Okay?"

"Very," Alex said, unable to say more than a word at a time. Within minutes, self-consciousness crept over him, the high wearing off as he realized he was covered in his own release and his pants were twisted around one ankle. As it dawned on him, he blushed. "Can I...uh...use your shower?" He glanced at his abs.

Nicholas straddled him and kissed him again, making sure Alex was watching as he dipped his head low and used a flat, gentle caress of his tongue to lap at Alex's skin, eyes never leaving his. "Yeah. You can if you want," he said, rocking back on his heels as he sat on Alex's legs. "You want help?"

"Sure," Alex said, smiling. He didn't want to leave the blanket fort without Nicholas, but he also hoped the shower would give him a good opportunity to take care of Nicholas's needs too.

Given the relatively neat appearance of the rest of Nicholas's apartment, Alex hadn't anticipated how cluttered the shower would be, the floor crowded with bottles. He could barely step inside, let alone allow Nicholas in with him, but they managed somehow, and Nicholas handed him body wash when he stepped in, adjusting the temperature to be hot but not too hot. Alex took the bottle and read the label, snorting.

"Really? Gingerbread body wash? You know this works as well as any other soap, right?" He cradled the bottle and wrapped one arm in front of himself to hide his body, self-conscious. Nicholas having already seen him naked wasn't relevant. He'd never showered with anyone before, and the experience a little overwhelming, considering how close they had to stand in the crowded space.

Nicholas grabbed the bottle and opened it, waving the shower gel under Alex's nose. "That's why I have it. Not because it works differently."

Alex rolled his eyes, but gave in. "Fine, okay. It smells really good."

"How's the water?"

"Perfect," Alex said, sighing, enjoying the warmth of the water and the scent of the body wash and the intimacy of the moment. "Tell me, does your shampoo smell like eggnog?" He was continuing the joke in hopes Nicholas wouldn't see how nervous he was. He wasn't nervous in the sense of not wanting to be there, but instead, with anticipation. There was a huge difference between the nudity in the intimate moment they'd shared, and in the nakedness of standing here and thinking about what it meant to have someone else in the shower with him.

"Eggnog? Ew, gosh, no. It's peppermint," Nicholas corrected him. Alex looked at the floor, unable to figure out which of the half-empty bottles was shampoo, but Nicholas reached down without a second glance and picked the container up from the center, squeezing some into his palm. "This isn't seasonal. They sell it all the time. Turn."

The command was gentle and Alex obliged, letting Nicholas nudge him into place before gently massaging the mint shampoo into Alex's scalp for him, letting the pads of his fingers work it in softly. "It tingles," Alex said. He was whisper quiet over the sound of water streaming down their bodies. Tilting his head back so Nicholas had easier access, he gave into the touch, then stopped trying to cover himself. His arms fell to his sides, and his shoulders relaxed. A moment later, he took a half step back and leaned his head on Nicholas's shoulder. The new angle made Nicholas washing his hair impossible, but that didn't matter. They were relishing in the closeness of things, with Nicholas sweeping suds from his forehead, away from his eyes, pressing a kiss to his temple. Alex turned more in an effort to get more contact, a better kiss, and a moan escaped his lips as he reached behind himself to pull Nicholas close. Nicholas hardened against his lower back, pressing against him, and he reached back, sliding his hand up Nicholas's leg to pull him closer. Anything to feel more, really. More touch. More kisses. More everything.

Alex kept angling his head for kisses, but Nicholas finally turned him to make contact easier. Their wet bodies were slick against each other as they kissed and since Alex was shorter than Nicholas, there was no way Alex could miss how hard he was, with Nicholas pressed against his stomach. The closeness and intimacy made Alex realize how he'd been standoffish in part to avoid this, being vulnerable with someone else. He hadn't been avoiding others so they couldn't have him, but instead so he wouldn't know what he was missing. Now, he knew what he'd held himself back from for so long, and this time he wasn't avoiding the touch. He leaned in and gave into having Nicholas right there, their hands on each other's skin.

Nicholas cupped his face and kissed him, rinsing the suds from his hair. As Alex tried to reach for the shampoo bottle and return the favor, he watched Nicholas use his foot to scoot it away so Alex couldn't. "Later," he said.

Alex wasn't sure when Nicholas had grabbed it again, but he could smell the gingerbread body wash as he slathered it on Alex's body, starting at his shoulders and working his way down. He focused on Alex's abs after, and

Alex hoped he could still feel the strength there instead of the layer of holiday sweets he'd put on. Nicholas's hands slipped to Alex's back and massaged his spine before grabbing his ass again, letting the soap and water give him the slickness he needed for his fingers to press against and gently inside of Alex.

Alex was struggling to stay standing, to not come unglued. Everything about the moment undid him in the best ways. His lips grazed Nicholas's neck as he leaned against him for support, kissing his jaw. If he had worried in any way that this was just sex and not an indication of more, the fear was gone now. There was tenderness in the way Nicholas cared for him, washed him, the most intimate acts together that they could possibly get. Alex was weak at the knees, literally.

He sank to the floor as a result, shifting to keep his balance and trying not to slip in the water and suds. The smattering of bottles toppled behind and beside him. "Dang it," Nicholas said, "hold on a second." He put a hand on Alex's chest, placing him on pause. The direction things were heading in was very clear, and the last thing either of them wanted was to kill the moment because of some clutter, but with the bottles there, they couldn't keep going. Nicholas scooped them up and opened the glass shower door with an elbow, shoving them unceremoniously onto the floor. Alex followed suit, grabbing some and tossing them out, too, until the floor of the shower was clean and the other side was decidedly not.

"I swear I'm cleaning your shower out after this," Alex groaned. "We're getting rid of everything you don't use every day because next time, I'm not stopping for clutter removal." His hands slid up Nicholas's thigh as he tried to will himself to focus on what they'd been doing before. The words *next time* rattled in his brain. There hadn't been a this time yet, but already Alex was sure they'd have more experiences like this.

Alex pulled him closer, using one hand to stroke Nicholas as he ran his tongue along his length. It didn't matter the water streamed down their bodies, pooling in his mouth as he focused on every part of Nicholas. Instead, he used the water as an asset to make his mouth wetter and warmer when wrapping his lips around Nicholas. He stayed close, gripping Nicholas's thighs to take him deeper, his head bobbing forward, slowly at first to figure out what he should be doing, how to go about this in a way that was good for Nicholas, before he picked up the pace. The shower water masked his watering eyes well, and Nicholas's hands grazed his scalp as they played with his hair, not to rub shampoo in, but to provide leverage.

It didn't take him long to discover he didn't have much of a gag reflex, and if he did, he suppressed it well, letting Nicholas thrust into his mouth as he whimpered and moaned around him. One of his hands gripped Nicholas's ass firmly, the other palming at his own sudden need. Nicholas caressed the back of his neck gently with one hand, using the other to stabilize himself against the shower wall as he leaned back. Alex didn't flinch and didn't waver his eye contact in spite of the water, watching Nicholas for a reaction and figuring out what pushed his buttons so he could repeat them. He learned fast, judging by the sounds Nicholas made, and Alex was reassured he was doing well despite his lack of experience.

What surprised him was how he could feel Nicholas getting closer, not by his words and moans and how he moaned Alex's name—though those things all helped—but by the way Nicholas involuntarily jerked in his hand and mouth, the way he twitched for release. Alex pulled him deep, knowing what was about to happen as he took Nicholas again. He silently begged for Nicholas to let go, to let it happen and let Alex taste the fruits of his labor. Nicholas did, and only afterward he pulled Alex back up to kiss him. "You're good. You're so, so good. Jeez, Alex, I…" He didn't seem to know what else to say, and he didn't have to say anything else because after that he kissed Alex, pressing him against the wall and biting his lower lip, working his mouth to Alex's neck. "You're so sexy. Oh gosh, you're beautiful and perfect and good…" he muttered.

Alex found himself sucking at Nicholas's neck, his chest and collarbone, leaving a trail of marks on his skin. They were sure to stick around. "You know I'm not going to hide those, right?"

"What?" Alex mumbled, lips pressed to his chest.

"I'm going to put on the deepest V-neck shirt in my closet, show all these off so everyone knows what you stole from me."

"What'd I steal?" Alex pulled back, puzzled.

"My heart. Obviously."

"Oh my God. Just when I thought you couldn't get any cheesier." Alex laughed and reached for the door of the shower.

Nicholas grabbed his arm and pulled him in for a kiss. "You like cheese."

Alex did, in fact, like the cheesiness a lot, and he didn't mind if Nicholas showed off the marks he'd left. *Let him,* he thought. Let Nicholas show everyone he had marked him, claimed him, taken his heart and made them both believe in something bigger than the season that had threatened to keep them apart. This wasn't lust, in spite of how they'd been tangled up in each other in the fort and the shower. It came from a place deep in Alex's soul, some place of intense longing, and he knew he was falling fast and hard for Nicholas. Inescapable and inevitable, Alex didn't stop himself from the fall.

That night, Alex didn't try to leave. He stayed, wearing his pajama pants and some sheets draped over him. They'd eaten popcorn and half watched other movies, talking instead of giving the movies their full attention. Nicholas couldn't be sure when or how, but the conversation starting with "What music do you like?" and "What do you want to do after grad school?" had become "We should make a blanket fort next Christmas too," and "You're going to have to teach me how to build a snowman so I don't look ridiculous next year." There was an implication they'd have another Christmas, another winter, an entire year together ahead obvious in the plans they made.

"Seriously, I have to go home," Alex said, still tangled in sheets a day and a half later. He wasn't actively trying to untangle himself, instead just stating facts.

"Why?"

"Because I haven't had a proper shower in three days. Or changed clothes."

"You haven't worn your clothes half the time, so they're not bad. And you have showered a couple of times. With me, remember?"

"I meant a real shower, with soap and shampoo and no handsome guys to distract me," Alex lamented. He chuckled right after, never minding the distraction

Nicholas offered. He could imagine Alex would want to take a proper shower, brush his teeth with more than toothpaste on his finger in a pinch. "Besides. I don't want to overstay my welcome."

"Fine," Nicholas sighed. He held tightly to Alex's hand. "Come back right afterward so I can welcome you all over again?"

"I *have to*, don't I?" Alex snarked. "We have a party to set up for." He'd said "have to" like setting up would be a chore, but the sarcasm was apparent.

"You do have to. We should take the fort down too. I don't think my back can handle another night on the floor," Nicholas groaned.

"I swear, you're an old man. *The Holiday* and now back pain?" Alex kissed him. "That's okay. I haven't gotten to see if your bed is as comfortable as you promised."

Nicholas giggled. "You're right. So come back, we'll have a party, and then you can test my mattress as soon as everyone leaves." With one more kiss, Alex finally managed to pull himself away.

Chapter Fifteen

Midnight

Alex tried to force himself to stay away the full two hours he had said he'd be gone. If for no other reason, the time might help to give himself a little space to think and to give Nicholas some time alone. But his undistracted shower hadn't taken fifteen minutes. Fifteen *including* a good shave.

He needed to kill time to avoid looking desperate. Even though he assumed no potential employers would be sending emails between Christmas and New Year's, he sat down to check them anyway. As expected, all he had was spam—ads for postholiday discounts at all the larger stores. Hoping to delay himself further, he pulled out his phone. Browsing Instagram was a good way to make himself wait a few more minutes, but as he opened the app, a text from Nicholas appeared at the top of the screen.

When are you coming back? ;)

At least Alex didn't need to worry about looking desperate by going back earlier than expected. Clearly, they were on the same page, wanting to be in one place, no hallway between them. He tapped out a quick reply.

You can't possibly miss me already. I just left. How'd you get my number? >:-O

Alex reasonably assumed Nicholas had gotten his number the same way he'd gotten Nicholas's—from Jade. Neither one had sent a text before now, and he'd been out of commission, phone-wise, until a few days after Christmas.

What do you mean I can't miss you? Is there some kind of rule against it?

Alex laughed out loud at that one, only to be interrupted by another text before he could respond.

Bring your toothbrush so you don't have to leave next time.

If I'm there too much, you'll get sick of me.

Before Alex could put his phone away again, it vibrated with one last message: *Never.*

Alex sighed and looked at the time on his phone. He'd been in his own apartment for less than an hour, but he couldn't resist or wait any longer. Instead, he grabbed a change of clothes, his toothbrush, and a few DVDs. He also included the unopened peppermint bark Nicholas had given him on the day they met. Though his apartment was right across the hall, leaving Nicholas to come back to change his clothes or brush his teeth was as silly to him as it apparently seemed to Nicholas.

When Alex walked across the hall, he suddenly wondered how to go in. Nicholas was expecting him, so knocking seemed strange, but they hadn't established whether or not he could enter unprompted. He stood at the door for a minute, then lifted his hand and knocked. Nicholas yanked the door open, then blinked. "I thought you were a delivery person or a door-to-door salesman. What the heck are you knocking for?"

"It's polite to knock," Alex said. "I figured it was rude to let myself—" Nicholas cut him off with a kiss.

"Next time, come on in. *Mi casa es*...whatever. Just come in. What's that?" he gestured to the stuff under Alex's arm.

"You said to bring my toothbrush, so I figured you wouldn't mind me bringing my clothes for the party?"

"No, I meant *that*," Nicholas said, pointing at the DVD cases sandwiched between his clothes and arm. Alex held up the obviously old and well-loved DVD case for Nicholas to see.

"It's my favorite Christmas movie."

"I hate to break this to you, but your favorite Christmas movie's a Halloween movie."

"It very, very clearly says Christmas in the title," Alex said. "Besides. I watched your favorites. Turnabout is fair play, sir."

"I've *seen* your favorite. I watch it every year. On Halloween. Where it belongs." Nicholas took the movie and put it on the DVD player for them to watch later. They agreed in that sense: streaming was inferior. Both of them liked having a DVD, a physical tangible object to put in the player. Neither of them knew why. They simply knew they were on the same page there.

"If you don't like that one, we can watch my second-favorite Christmas movie," Alex said.

"If that's your first choice, do I even want to know what your second favorite is?" He laughed and then looked at him seriously. "I'll bite. What is it?"

"*Die Hard.*" Alex had to bite his lip to stifle his laughter over Nicholas's expression. Confusion and surprise were written on his face.

"You can't be serious right now. I thought the biggest issue you had with my Christmas movie choices was how straight they were, and you pick a hardcore action film?"

Nicholas raised his eyebrow.

"Okay, consider this: sweaty Bruce Willis in a tank top. That movie was basically my gay awakening."

"Fine, okay. That's fair," Nicholas said. "You're still really, really weird."

Alex did his best to make himself at home, but he didn't know any of the protocol on staying at someone's place multiple times in the context of romance. He put his toothbrush in the bathroom beside Nicholas's, and placed his change of clothes on top of the dresser. They'd have to get ready for the party later, but the plan was to decorate first.

"Here," Alex said, returning to the kitchen and passing the peppermint bark to Nicholas.

"Is this...?" Nicolas ran his finger along a crumpled corner, the same corner that had gotten banged up when he'd dropped the box in the parking lot in a mad dash to give it to Alex before he left.

"It is."

"Thought this was for your friend," Nicholas said, winking.

"Then I guess I'll need to share with my friend," Alex said. "Want some peppermint bark, friend?"

"I'm your friend, huh?" Nicholas asked. He wasn't sure he'd use friendship as the right word for how they'd spent the last few days, unable to keep their hands off each other, but he couldn't resist pushing Alex's buttons. Alex's eyes twinkled mischievously.

"Are you saying we're not friends? I'm offended," Alex pouted. He knew all too well they were far more than that by now, but Nicholas tackled him to the couch anyway, pinning him and kissing him. "What would you call it?" Alex asked, struggling to flip them and gain the upper hand to pin Nicholas instead. Nicholas didn't allow him to, and their wrestling match became peppered with kisses and pokes in the ribs.

"A whole hell of a lot more than what you're suggesting," Nicholas said. Alex slid the shirt off of Nicholas. The second it hit the floor, Nicholas shifted back to give Alex room to remove his own. He pinned Alex, wrists in his hands as he held him to the couch and nipped at his lip. "We can be anything you want us to be," he added. What they called it didn't matter as long as they got to keep doing *this*. Nicholas sat up again, shifting his weight to Alex's thighs as he unbuttoned his jeans, tugging them down around his knees and kissing his way down Alex's body.

"Holy crap!" Jade exclaimed, spotting them as soon as she opened the door without knocking. She nearly dropped the champagne bottle in her hands, squeezing her eyes shut and turning around. "Get a room!"

"We *had* a room," Nicholas said. "You chose to enter it." He chuckled and moved off Alex, watching him scramble for clothing as his cheeks turned red. He leaned in close and whispered in his ear. "It's okay. She's teasing."

"Uh, hi, Jade," Alex said sheepishly, putting his shirt back on after fastening his jeans so she could turn around and put the champagne bottle down. She was looking everywhere but at him as she regained her bearings, having seen far more of her new neighbor than either of them anticipated she should. She needed the opportunity to unsee that.

"I can always come back later if you two are busy," she said. "When you said we were setting up for the party at three, I was pretty sure you meant you wanted me here at, y'know...three."

Nicholas had lost track of the time. Over the past few days, time had passed in a blur, hours marked by whatever meal they ate at the moment, time marked by kisses and whimpers and moans and movies. Clocks and calendars hadn't mattered at all until they'd realized, rather suddenly, New Year's Eve had arrived. They'd forgotten entirely until Jade texted to ask when to set up.

"We can set up now. It's fine," Alex said. He was still trying to calm his blush. Even if Jade did leave and come back later, he wasn't sure he could continue what they started without embarrassment.

"I'll uh...start knocking from now on," Jade said. Alex understood why. As much as she seemed to want them to be happy and at ease, she probably didn't need to ever see them that happy or at ease again.

"Nobody invited Sean, right?" Nicholas asked. The last thing he needed was an unexpected surprise, and if he *was* coming, he needed time to talk to Alex alone and let him know he was never revisiting his last relationship. Ever. He wasn't going to kick Sean out of a party—he wasn't that kind of guy—but he certainly wasn't interested in having Sean in his life after what had happened at the last party.

"No. He's at his partner's parents' place up north for the weekend," Jade said. He sighed audibly, relieved, and Nicholas didn't miss her glance toward the door to be sure Alex hadn't come back from his apartment, where he'd gone to fetch more glasses for the toast. "What's the deal with you and Alex?"

"Oh, things are absolutely awful with him, as you can tell," Nicholas said, smirking. He stuck cake-pop sticks into the balls of cake he'd rolled earlier. "What you walked in on earlier? We were, uh, cage fighting. No romance here."

"Yeah. I can tell you two really hate each other," she said. "Considering this place would still look like some sort of weird blanket palace, had I not intervened. Someone has to keep you on track with the decorations, apparently." She gestured at everything they had gotten done, the gold and silver streamers that had replaced the blanket fort and the Christmas tree, and plenty of party poppers scattered around for easy access later. "Seriously, what's the deal with you two?"

Nicholas was thinking about denying his intense feelings, but Jade wasn't stupid. They'd barely stopped looking at each other all afternoon, and after the tree was down, Alex had gone to change his clothes, with Nicholas following to see if he "needed help." There was no point in acting like this was only friendship. "We're figuring things out as we go along," he said.

"When's the last time he was at his place? Besides now, I mean?"

"Earlier today. Jeez, J, it isn't like he lives here!" Nicholas rolled his eyes, wondering if Alex living there *was* such a bad idea. The thought crossed his mind, but Nicholas had to remind himself they hadn't known each other very long. Even then, he thought maybe their relationship was a case of when you knew, you just...knew. With Alex, he felt certain.

"How long was he gone?"

Nicholas turned his back to her and focused on the cake pops, intently ignoring her.

"Nicholas. Seriously. How long was he gone?"

"About forty-five minutes." He didn't look at her.

"Jesus, Nick, forty-five minutes? After being here for three days?"

At first, Nicholas wanted to call her a hypocrite. With Veronica, she'd gone on two dates before giving her a key. Sometimes the feelings were simply right. Her laugh stopped him. Either way, he got the point. Just because she'd been there and done that, didn't mean she wanted to see Nicholas get hurt, not after how things had blown up with Sean.

"I think I might love him." The words came out of his mouth easily, without second-guessing.

"I'm happy for you. Promise."

There was hesitation in her tone of voice, and Nicholas knew she didn't know Alex well enough to give her full blessing, but her words were enough to tell him she supported him regardless.

Alex leaned his head against Nicholas's shoulder. He was exhausted, struggling to stay awake until midnight. He assumed it had a lot to do with his sleep schedule being thoroughly screwed up from their overnight movie marathons. He knew he'd have to get his sleep back in shape before classes started the following week, but for now, he enjoyed the party from the couch. Even Nicholas—the ever-enthusiastic host—was more focused on Alex than the party, at least by 11:30.

Earlier, Jade had pulled him aside while Nicholas took a shower. She had mercifully reassured him Sean wouldn't crash this party like he had a couple of weeks before. Part of Alex's mind couldn't believe it had only been a few weeks. It felt like so much longer. Most of the rest of the conversation was Jade trying to feel him out to see what his intentions were. For as much as Nicholas claimed she was like a younger sister to him, she clearly had the opposite perception.

Alex had simply reassured her that he liked Nicholas a lot and then let her in on his insecurity about how and when to move the relationship forward. He wondered aloud if Nicholas saw him as a friend, or a friend with benefits, or the potential for something more. Alex had never spent time dating so, obviously, this wasn't his strong suit.

"Darlin'," Jade said, "you two won't get anywhere if you keep running your conversations through me. Tell him how you feel. I can't speak for him, but he told you to bring your toothbrush back. That's pretty significant."

"How did you know?" Alex asked her.

"He answered my text instead of yours by accident. I was wondering why he told me to bring my toothbrush, but it isn't hard to figure out who's toothbrush he wants here."

Now, with Nicholas's arm around him, the party continued around them. He thought maybe Jade could be right. "You doing okay?" Nicholas asked, leaning in and kissing his forehead.

"I'm great," Alex said, lifting his head and smiling. "A little sleepy."

"Think you can hold out for midnight?" Nicholas said. "It's only a few more minutes."

"Yeah," Alex said, sitting up straighter and blinking. Jade was pouring glasses of champagne, preparing for the toast. She'd already told them to stay put on the couch, that she could do the work. He was grateful for her, both now as she did that, and earlier for the reassurances she'd given him. He didn't know what the next year held for him, but if his last few weeks were any indication of the year ahead, it would be surprising and sweet. He knew beyond all of that, there was no one he'd rather ring in the new year with.

As he stood to get champagne for them, Nicholas followed, one hand on Alex's waist the whole way. Everyone gathered around, glasses in hand, as they counted down the dying seconds of the year, with wild optimism, as they looked toward the future.

10

9

8

Alex thought about where he wanted to be this time next year. Something told him he'd be in the same room with the same people, Nicholas's hand on his waist. He hoped he was right.

7

6

5

Everything about the past year had been a wild and crazy ride. He'd faced heartbreak, and he'd moved across the country. He'd been accepted to grad school and made new friends. There was a distinct possibility he'd met the love of his life. That was a lot to process.

4

3

2

Nicholas's hand grazed his cheek, cupping his chin to lift it as he looked into his eyes.

1

As Nicholas kissed him for what had to be the millionth time since they'd first kissed two weeks before, in the same room, surrounded by most of the same people, he was sure of one thing: they were starting this year together, and he could feel the love and joy and comfort deep within himself. He'd be ending the year with Nicholas too. He'd had no clue, when they'd made their move under the mistletoe, that the kiss they'd shared then had been Alex's last first-ever kiss.

Chapter Sixteen

A New Start

It took nearly an hour and a half for all the guests to wander back to their own apartments or head home for the night. Alex had stared at the clock and struggled to keep his eyes open at all, even after he caught a second wind, reinvigorated with thoughts about the year ahead. It didn't matter, though. Once they left, he and Nicholas were the only people in the apartment again.

"So. Our midnight kiss," Nicholas said.

"What about it?"

"It was nice. But there were a lot of people around, right?" he asked.

"Of course there were. It was *your* party."

"Our party. I thought we could have a do-over," Nicholas said. "Now that we're alone."

"Yeah?" Alex asked. He stepped closer and let Nicholas wrap his arms around him. The music from the party was playing quietly—they hadn't turned it off yet—and Nicholas swayed him gently. "A do-over? Okay. Ten...nine...eight..." He started to count down.

"Seven...six...five..." Nicholas joined in and they counted in unison. Alex couldn't miss Nicholas speeding up at the end, mostly in hopes of getting to the kiss faster. "Four, three, two..."

Without either of them saying one, Nicholas's lips were on his. His hands gripped Alex close, and he walked them backward, tugging Alex with him toward the bedroom he'd more than once promised held a soft, luxurious bed. They could barely keep their lips off each other.

Nicholas turned them without Alex paying much mind, and Nicholas guided him down onto the bed. "Do you make wishes at midnight?"

"Maybe," Alex said. "Why, do you? What'd you wish for?"

"Another year of this," Nicholas confessed. "I really like you, Alex."

"I like you too." Alex didn't say all of what he felt in the moment, but he did pull Nicholas closer, hands on his stomach to ruck up his shirt and guide it off. The sound of fireworks and celebrations had all long faded now, around two in the morning, but they rang in the new beginning in the right way, with Nicholas's body on his, sliding his clothes off too. "I want you," Alex breathed the words, a quiet confession in a quiet room.

"Are you sure?" he asked quietly. Alex nodded. "I want you too, Alex. I have since you said you hated peppermint."

"I don't really hate it," Alex confessed.

His eyes crinkling with a smile, Nicholas said, "I know. I was joking. But I've wanted to be close to you since then anyway." His hands were on Alex, lips on his body, and on the first day of the new year, in a dark room, with Nicholas guiding him every step of the way, Alex gave them what they both wanted. Nicholas sank onto him, whimpering as Alex filled him, and Alex had never experienced something like this—not physically, at least—

in his entire life. He was in heaven, his body burning. He could barely believe he wasn't dreaming—some sleep-induced early-December haze. But this *was* real, and more real with each time he moved in Nicholas, and more obvious with every time Nicholas moaned his name, told him how good he felt, how perfect this was.

He didn't last long before Nicholas was falling onto him, kissing him, breathing him in and holding him close. He didn't move until Nicholas rolled off and held him close. "Hey, Alex?"

"Yeah?"

"That was amazing."

"Yeah," Alex agreed. He nodded and tried to compose himself again, but his second wind was gone and he drifted off, naked and barely covered by sheets, Nicholas's limbs tangled with his own. Of all of the ways to start the new year, this was unexpected, but also the best way he could imagine.

The next morning, he awoke to bacon again, and he wondered how long breakfast in bed would be sustainable from Nicholas. It made sense in a new relationship, something done to impress someone, forgotten after a while, but he didn't care if it died down a little later. For now, Alex wanted to make sure Nicholas knew he appreciated the effort. They had a long time to show each other how much they cared in other ways, but right now he wanted his hands, mouth, and body on Nicholas again. He'd fix his sleep schedule later, worry about everything else later. For the time being, he was focused on one thing and one thing only: his feelings for Nicholas.

"I have to go home today," Alex said. He'd have class any day now, and if he didn't at least attempt to find a job, he'd be right back where he'd been before: in California.

"Why?"

"I have to change clothes and go look for a job," Alex sighed. He hadn't been back to his apartment since New Year's Eve, aside from grabbing a change of clothes or a bottle of whiskey and coming back to Nicholas's place. "I can't freeload here all the time. At some point, I should probably buy some of the bacon."

"Yeah, okay," Nicholas sighed. His TA job didn't start for another few days, but as much as he hated to admit it, the break would be over soon. They'd have to find a new normal. Normal sleep. Normal time spent together. Normal showers and getting ready. "You coming over later?"

"You're not tired of me yet?" Alex asked. He leaned in for one more quick kiss.

"No. But, uh, I do have something for you," Nicholas said, watching as Alex fixed his hair in the mirror even though he'd inevitably end up redoing it when he got across the hall and changed.

"Yeah? Is it chocolate bark?" They'd polished off the box Nicholas gave him for Christmas a week ago.

"Nope," Nicholas said. He wrapped his arms around Alex's waist. "Just this." The clink of metal on the porcelain sink counter caught Alex's attention. A key.

"Are you serious?" Alex turning in Nicholas's arms.

"You're always here. I know I'm moving fast, but I want you to be here. I like having you here, and I want you to stay here. You...um...you obviously don't have to get rid of your place or anything. But I want you to know you can be here for anything, anytime." Barely disguised under the things Nicholas said, the offer was clear. Sure, he might not have been asking Alex to move in immediately, since neither of them knew what the new year would bring, how classes or jobs or their real lives that existed outside of the bubble of one holiday break could stress or even break them.

But it was a question. Nothing about this was about moving too fast or whether or not Alex was ready, or if they'd manage to work things out in spite of everything ahead. The gift of the key was to ask one very simple question: Are you in this like I'm in this?

"I'll be back later," Alex said, sliding the key on his key ring. "Want me to bring takeout?" That said everything needed.

Epilogue

Next Christmas

One year.

Three hundred and sixty-five days.

Alex could hardly believe so much time had passed since he'd run into Nicholas in the middle of a grocery store and squabbled about peppermint bark, but it had. He could never be thankful enough for their local grocery store and their understocked shelf. The past year had held so many beautiful memories. They'd shared late-night study sessions, soft kisses, more than a few arguments over how to build shelving units or dressers, and plenty of impromptu blanket forts they left up for days on end.

In May, Alex stopped pretending and got rid of his apartment for good, moving across the hall with the help of Brandon—who he'd finally gotten to meet—and Jade. In June, they'd taken a week-long vacation to visit his mother in California. Nicholas said he wished his mother was still alive so Alex could meet her. From what he'd said, Alex would have loved her, and it would have been mutual. For Thanksgiving, they stayed in Omaha, celebrating with Jade and Veronica. Between grad school and the IT internship he'd taken, Alex had gotten busy. Travel was harder than ever.

If the year behind them was any indication, Alex was right when he'd known Nicholas was the one. He was the only person Alex could picture spending a lifetime with. As he carefully rolled out cookie dough with Nicholas, preparing to take plates of treats to all their neighbors, Alex realized he was excited for Christmas for the first time in years. He looked forward to the small traditions they could create. They'd already made plans to watch their favorite Christmas movies—all four of them, including the one Nicholas insisted was for Halloween— in a blanket fort. They were waiting until after the Christmas party to set it up.

Instead of interrupting Nicholas's baking by being drunk and upset, like the year before, Alex was helping. Nicholas pinched off a piece of dough, feeding the bite to him, and he thought about how much things had changed. The year before, he hadn't been willing to come in for pie. This year, he literally ate from Nicholas's fingers.

But the night wasn't done, and as much as they still had to bake, Alex had other things to finish. "I'll be right back, babe," he said, washing his hands. "I realized I forgot to grab something at the store." He kissed Nicholas's cheek.

"Need me to come with you?"

"Nope. I can get it. I won't be long." The last thing Alex needed was for Nicholas to come with him, to catch him in a lie about where he was headed. Instead, Alex pulled out his phone and texted Jade.

Can you cover for me? Headed outside now.

Was that tonight? Shoot, I totally forgot.

A cold chill ran down Alex's spine. The entire plan was dependent on making sure Nicholas stayed away from the window, and Jade had forgotten? Before he could send a panicked reply, his phone buzzed with another message.

I'm messing with you. On my way up. Your stuff is in the laundry room.

Alex was lucky to have Jade on his side. Downstairs, he found the bag she'd hung on a hook in the shared basement laundry room. He used to stash gifts in his apartment, but now they lived together, so he couldn't. She had become his go-to for hiding them. He slung the bag over his shoulder and walked into the frigid air, wearing the coat and gloves Nicholas had loaned him a season before.

This time around, finding the right place to build a snowman was easier. As he reached into the snow, he was thankful it had fallen to give him the help he needed. He started packing it together to form a ball. He'd had a plan B, one involving a store-bought snowman, but this was like real magic, the one that would prove to Nicholas how special he was.

Upstairs, Jade knocked on the door. She didn't need to, since Alex was outside in the snow, but Nicholas didn't know she knew that, so she knocked anyway. When Nicholas answered, she stepped in and feigned cluelessness. "Where's Alex?"

"He ran to the store," he said. His apron was covered with flour, with some in his beard and on his cheek.

"Need some help?"

"Sure," he answered. She distracted him, helping him fill the cookies with bacon. When she reached for the last set, Nicholas grabbed them. "Not those. I need them for something else."

"Ooh, okay. We got a vegan on the hall?"

"No. You'll see. It isn't a big deal." He was defensive, and he tried to dial back his tone. It wasn't that he didn't want Jade to know. He just wanted Alex to know *first*.

"Okay," she said, shrugging. She used whatever small talk she had at her disposal to keep him talking, focused on conversation and away from the window until her phone buzzed. "Oh, shoot, Veronica needs me. Dinner emergency!" She rushed out the door without another word.

Nicholas looked down at the final cookie, which he hadn't filled yet. He took a deep breath and started to assemble and fill it, hoping he had enough time to finish decorating before Alex returned. Of all the treats he'd made, that was the only one he wanted to be sure was perfect.

As soon as Alex got inside, Nicholas thrust the cookie toward him. "I made this while you were gone."

"It looks amazing, babe," Alex said. "I'll eat it later, okay?" He shifted back and forth, hands in his pockets. "Can't you eat it now?"

"Can it wait a second, sweetheart? We need to talk first." His tone of voice was intense and pleading, and Nicholas wondered for a second if he'd misread everything. Maybe the cookie was the opposite of what he should have done. His heart sank, and he started to feel a sense of panic.

"Okay. What's going on?" Nicholas asked, taking a deep breath and putting the cookie on a plate behind him. If this went horribly wrong, if for some reason Alex was breaking up with him, or moving out, or going back to California, he wanted to make sure Alex forgot the cookie existed.

But Alex took his hands, walking backward to the window and bringing Nicholas with him as he spoke. "We've had a good year together, haven't we?" Alex asked.

Nicholas nodded as a lump formed in his throat. Now, he was absolutely positive they'd been on different pages, and this was the end. But Alex kept talking.

"I can't imagine anyone I'd rather have spent the year with. You've been amazing. You're *always* amazing, and I'm so, so in love with you," Alex said. "Nicholas, love of my life, I want to spend every year with you from now on."

"Wait, what?" Nicholas's brain was catching up with the words Alex said, and he wasn't positive he was hearing him correctly.

"I have something I want you to see." Alex opened the curtains and Nicholas looked out the window, down to the snow. There stood a lopsided snowman—Alex had yet to perfect his technique—with a sign hanging from its neck.

"Are you being serious right now?" Nicholas asked, voice quivering as he turned back to see Alex on one knee, an open ring box in his hand. The box held a wood-and-gold ring that suited Nicholas's tastes perfectly.

"I'm dead serious. You're the one, Nicholas. I want to spend my life with you. If you'll have me, of course."

"Oh my gosh. You couldn't have eaten the cookie, could you?" Nicholas lamented, walking away without answering, leaving Alex on one knee.

"Wait, you're rejecting me over a cookie? I'm asking you to marry me, and you're upset I didn't eat it yet?" Alex furrowed his brow. He'd spent an hour in the snow building a snowman, and weeks planning the perfect proposal, and Nicholas was more focused on a bacon-filled treat. He wondered if this was a weird way of letting him down easy.

"Open it! You don't even have to eat it, but open it. Please!"

The top of the cookie was beautifully frosted with Alex's name, small hearts piped around the edges. Alex took the cookie and sighed, twisting off the top layer. Inside was a thin silver ring. "Oh my gosh," he breathed.

"Alex, will you marry me?"

Had anyone been outside next to the snowman Alex had built, they would have been able to look up and see Alex nod, see his lips form the word *yes*, and see him kiss Nicholas as Nicholas lifted him into his arms. But no one was there to see them except the snowman, the sign hanging from his neck, blowing in the winter breeze, a question written in thick, black letters:

Nicholas, will you marry me?

Nicholas's Holiday Recipes

Mr. Grinch Cocktail

1 oz. Midori
1 ½ oz. lemon lime soda
½ oz. lime juice
Ice
Maraschino cherry with stem
Corn syrup and green sanding sugar

Rim martini glass or 4 oz. mason jar with corn syrup and green sanding sugar. Place cherry with stem in the bottom of the glass.

Shake Midori and lime juice with ice.

Strain into glass, top with lemon lime soda, and serve.

Virginize by substituting alcohol with 1 ½ oz. melon sports drink.

Homemade Salted Caramels

1 c. melted butter
2 c. packed brown sugar
1 c. granulated sugar
1 c. light corn syrup
1 can evaporated milk
1 pint heavy whipping cream
2 tsp. sea salt
2 tsp. vanilla extract

Melt butter in large pot (must be large as mixture will increase in size).

Add sugars and corn syrup, stirring until combined.

Add vanilla and sea salt, then stir.

Bring mixture up to 247-250°F, stirring every 1-2 minutes and being sure to scrape down corners and sides to prevent crystals from forming.

Pour into parchment-lined baking dish. Sprinkle with additional sea salt if desired.

Cool on counter for 15 minutes, then in refrigerator for 15 minutes. Slice while firm but pliable, using a hot knife.

Surprise Bacon-Filled Maple Cookies

5 ½ c. all-purpose flour
1 tsp. salt
4 sticks (2 c.) butter, at room temperature
1 ½ c. sugar
½ c. pure maple syrup
½ tsp. maple extract
1 egg yolk
1 egg, beaten
Royal icing in red and in green
1 lb. cooked bacon

Sift together flour and salt.

In a separate bowl, cream butter and sugar until light and fluffy.

Add egg yolk, maple syrup, and maple extract to butter mixture until well-combined.

Add flour mixture gradually, mixing until a thick dough forms.

Flatten dough, wrap in cling wrap, and refrigerate at least one hour until dough is firm to the touch.

Preheat oven to 350°.

On a floured surface, roll dough to 1/4 in. thickness.

Cut 2 whole circles and 2 donut-type circles for each cookie (donut-type circles are cookies with the center cut out, which will later be filled with bacon)

Brush each cookie piece with beaten egg, then bake for 10 minutes at 350°.

Cool completely.

On the top of the bottom-most cookie, pipe a circle of royal icing. Place one cookie with hole in it on top of the whole cookie. Make another circle of royal icing and place another cookie with a hole on top. Fill hole with diced bacon.

Make another ring of royal icing, placing a whole cookie (no hole) on top. Let dry.

Decorate with royal icing.

Salted Caramel Cocoa Syrup

1 stick (1/2 c.) butter
1 c. granulated sugar
2 tsp. sea salt
¼ c. unsweetened cocoa powder
1 pint heavy whipping cream
Milk
Desired toppings (caramel, chocolate, sea salt)
Coffee (optional)

In saucepan over medium heat, melt butter.

Add sugar and salt, stirring until dissolved, and bring mixture to a simmer.

Heat for 5 minutes, stirring often.

Add in cocoa powder and mix until combined.

Slowly add room temperature whipping cream and whisk until smooth.

Cook 5 more minutes. Cool slightly before serving.

To serve, mix ¼ c. warm syrup with 8 oz. warm milk (or warm milk and coffee, or just coffee). Top with desired toppings and enjoy.

Makes 12 servings of salted caramel cocoa syrup.

White Chocolate Raspberry Cake Pops

1 vanilla cake, baked and crumbled
Vanilla frosting (enough to make a play dough texture
    from the cake and frosting mix—about ½ container)
½ c. frozen raspberries
White chocolate, melted
Dark chocolate, melted (if desired)
1-2 tsp. coconut oil

Combine cake and frosting until mixture is moldable and forms a play dough consistency.

Add in frozen raspberries and shape mixture into balls about 1 to 1 ½ inches in diameter.

Dip cake pop stick into white chocolate and insert into cake pop. Place cake pops in freezer 1-2 hours until firm and cold.

Dip balls in white chocolate. Top with desired toppings, like drizzles of dark chocolate.

Serve chilled.

Kiss Under the Mistletoe Shots

(Makes 10 shots)

Rim tall shot glasses with dark chocolate syrup and peppermint pieces.

In a blender, combine 1 scoop chocolate ice cream, 1 oz. Bailey's, 1 tsp. dark chocolate syrup, and 1 tsp. peppermint bits. Fill each shot glass 1/3 full. Place in freezer while second layer is being prepared.

Rinse blender and combine 1 scoop peppermint ice cream, 1 oz. Bailey's, and 1 T. peppermint bits. Remove shot glasses from freezer and fill another 1/3. Place back in freezer.

Rinse blender and combine 1 scoop vanilla ice cream, 1 oz. Bailey's, and 2 oz. safe-to-eat sugar cookie dough. Blend, remove shot glasses from freezer, and fill shot glasses.

Top with whipped cream, chocolate syrup, and peppermint bits.

To virginize, substitute coffee creamer for Bailey's in recipe.

Holly Candy

3 T. butter
10 oz. marshmallows or mini marshmallows
5 c. cornflakes
Green food coloring
Red hot candy or red M&Ms

In a saucepan over medium heat, melt butter and add marshmallows, stirring until melted. Stir in food coloring and remove from heat.

Stir in cornflakes.

Drop by tablespoon onto parchment paper and decorate with 3 red hot candies or 3 red M&Ms.

Cranberry Orange Spritz

3 c. cranberry juice (unsweetened, not the juice cocktail
    kind)
2 c. orange juice
1 bottle (750 ml) vodka
1 ½ c. lemon juice
1 c. sugar
2 c. cranberry ginger ale (or regular ginger ale)

In a punch bowl, combine all ingredients except ginger ale. Chill. Top with ginger ale and serve by the cupful with orange slices and sugared cranberries.

Make sugared cranberries, the day before. Pour 2 c. cranberries onto a baking sheet, arranging them side-by-side in a single layer. In a saucepan, boil 1 c. water with 1 ½ c. sugar. Boil for 5-10 minutes to reduce to syrup. Let cool for 10 minutes before pouring over cranberries. Let soak overnight. Drain off excess syrup, then toss cranberries with 1 c. sugar. Dry on a pan at room temperature until ready to serve.

16 servings.

To virginize, omit vodka.

Turkey Vegetable Soup

1 stick (1/2 c.) butter
1 medium onion, diced
4 cloves garlic, minced
1 tsp salt
½ tsp. pepper
⅓ c. flour
1 carton (32 oz.) chicken broth
3 c. water
2 medium potatoes, diced
3 carrots, chopped small
3 stalks celery, chopped small
2 c. frozen corn
1 c. chopped cooked turkey or chicken
1 qt. half and half

In bottom of large stock pot, melt butter. Add onion, garlic, salt, and pepper, stirring often until onion is translucent. Add flour, stirring until thick.

Add broth, stirring to dissolve flour mixture.

Add vegetables and bring to boil. Allow to boil 20-30 minutes until vegetables are tender. Add half and half. Add additional seasonings to taste.

Simmer 20-30 minutes longer, serving hot.

Turkey Potato Pot Pie

Crusts for a 2-crust pie
⅓ c. butter or margarine
1 T. minced onion
½ tsp. minced garlic
½ tsp. salt
¼ tsp. pepper
⅓ c. flour
16 oz. chicken broth
½ c. milk
2 ½ c. shredded turkey (may substitute chicken)
2 ½ c. potatoes, diced, small
1 c. shredded carrots
1 pkg. frozen sweet corn

Place crusts in pie plates and preheat oven to 425°.

In a saucepan over medium heat, melt butter with seasonings.

Add in flour, stirring until thick.

Slowly add chicken broth and milk, stirring often until bubbly and thickened.

Sir in turkey, potatoes, carrots, and corn, then spoon filling into crust.

Place top crust over filling, cutting a vent in the crust.

Bake for 20-25 minutes until crust is golden and potatoes are tender.

If saving for the freezer, do not bake. Place pie in airtight storage and save for up to one month.

Corn Casserole

2 sticks butter (1 c.) butter, melted
4 eggs, beaten
6 oz. sour cream
2 cans whole kernel corn, drained.
2 cans cream corn
16 oz. corn muffin mix

Pour melted butter into casserole dish.

Add eggs and sour cream, mixing thoroughly.

Add cans of corn and muffin mix, stirring to combine (batter will be lumpy).

Bake for 1 hour and 15 minutes at 350°.

Recipe can be halved for a smaller amount; reduce baking time accordingly.

Double-Dipped French Toast

1 c. crushed cornflakes
½ c. steel-cut oatmeal
½ c. sugar
1 generous sprinkle cinnamon
2 eggs, beaten
½ c. milk
4 slices toast (yes, toasted, not bread)
Butter

In bowl, combine eggs and milk.

In separate bowl, combine cornflakes, oats, sugar, and cinnamon.

Dip toast into egg mixture, then into corn flake mixture, coating generously.

In skillet with melted butter, cook toast until golden brown and crispy.

Cut into halves or into triangles and serve with syrup and fresh fruit.

Times Square Cookie Pops

1 pkg. vanilla Oreos, crushed
1 pkg. cream cheese, softened (8 oz)
¼ c. melted white chocolate chips
Cake Pop Sticks
Vanilla frosting, melted
Silver, gold, or white sprinkles

Mix crushed cookies with softened cream cheese.

Roll mixture into balls.

Freeze balls. Dip cake pop sticks into melted white chocolate and insert into frozen cookie pops.

Return to freezer.

Melt frosting and dip frozen cake pops in melted frosting, tapping off excess, then roll in sprinkles.

Chill and serve.

Acknowledgements

When I was sixteen years old, a teacher and a librarian told me I'd never get a book to publication, that my writing wasn't good enough. This book isn't for them. This book *is* for everyone else who has heard the same thing. To all of you: keep writing.

Mostly, this book is for Zachary, who inspires me every single day. Zack, being your parent is a genuine joy. I can't imagine my life without you.

Mom, thank you for putting up with my Book Brain, and Toby, thank you for the hours spent at the pool so I could finish this. Jeffrey, I'm so proud of you. Carolin, Marius, Lucas, Nicholas, I love you. Gram, thank you for helping spark my love of reading. Granddad, I wish you could have been here to see this one.

Ally, I couldn't have done this without you saving my sanity on a regular basis. V+R forever.

Jaime, Skye, thank you for your input. Angelien, Kelsey, thank you for being there.

Jex, Em, Terri, Alex, Taylor, you told me to keep writing, so I did.

To the teachers who *did* believe: I couldn't have done this without your faith in me. To the Bean Coffee Co., thanks for fueling me with countless sandwiches and lattes, and for all of the encouraging words from their staff during my writing sessions.

Chef Joe DiPaolo, thank you for teaching me the trick to making the flakiest pie crust.

To everyone at NineStar Press, I'm so endlessly thankful you had faith in this story. Beth, DVPit is important and necessary, and without it, I'm not sure this would have happened as soon as it did.

To everyone who never got to live their truth, or are scared you won't be able to, I see you. I support you. And I hope you all find your Alex or Nicholas someday, if you want to.

About the Author

J R Hart is a queer thirtysomething novelist passionate about telling romantic and erotic stories about LGBT+ characters. When J R isn't writing, you can find her at the science museum with her son, cheering on her favorite soccer team, or at the Bean Coffee Co. plotting her next work. You can find her on Twitter and Instagram as @jrhartauthor or on her website at jrhartauthor.com.

Email: jrhartauthor@gmail.com

Twitter: @jrhartauthor

Website: www.jrhartauthor.com

Also Available from NineStar Press

Connect with NineStar Press

www.ninestarpress.com

www.facebook.com/ninestarpress

www.facebook.com/groups/NineStarNiche

www.twitter.com/ninestarpress

www.tumblr.com/blog/ninestarpress

www.ingramcontent.com/pod-product-compliance
Lightning Source LLC
Chambersburg PA
CBHW050518190726
48284CB00003B/848